CRY OF TERROR!

Cindy was turning to check on Joni when she slipped. Instinctively, her right hand shot out and grabbed a thick branch. It must have been dead and dried. It snapped, and she was falling. For the tiniest instant, just before the icy water engulfed her, Cindy thought she felt Bala's fingers touching her wrist.

Oh, God, no!

The cold was black and strong. She was going down and being swept backward. The fall had caught her without a solid breath. Her lungs screamed for air. She flailed blindly with her arms, her flesh cringing in the grip of the current. Her leg slapped a rock, then another. She kicked upward. Her head broke the surface.

"Alex!" Cindy screamed.

Books by Christopher Pike

LAST ACT
SPELLBOUND

Available from ARCHWAY Paperbacks

Spellbound

Christopher Pike

AN ARCHWAY PAPERBACK
Published by POCKET BOOKS
New York   London   Toronto   Sydney   Tokyo

AN ARCHWAY PAPERBACK *Original*

An Archway Paperback published by
POCKET BOOKS, a division of Simon & Schuster Inc.
1230 Avenue of the Americas, New York, N.Y. 10020

Copyright © 1988 by Christopher Pike
Cover artwork copyright © 1988 Brian Kotzky

ISBN: 0-671-64979-5

First Archway Paperback printing April 1988

10 9 8 7 6 5 4 3 2

AN ARCHWAY PAPERBACK and colophon are
registered trademarks of Simon & Schuster Inc.

Printed in the U.S.A.

IL 8+

For Eileen

Spellbound

CHAPTER

I

THE MORNING WAS BRISK as Cindy Jones stepped from her house to fetch the newspaper at the end of the driveway. She had grown up in the Rockies, but still the first breath of early mountain air always filled her with an invigorating freshness that was both surprising and pleasant. Dew glistened on the thick green branches of the many surrounding trees, evaporating swiftly in the bright sun. The sky was that special cerulean blue that longtime city dwellers could hardly imagine. It was going to be a beautiful day, she thought as she knelt and collected the paper, pulling off the rubber band and glancing at what was new in the small community of Timber, Wyoming.

An article that began in the lower right-hand corner of the second page changed her mind about what a beautiful day it was going to be.

HOW DID KAREN HOLLY DIE?
By Kent Cooke

Seven weeks ago today, on August 2, seventeen-year-old Karen Holly died. The circumstances surrounding her death, as reported by Jason Whitfield, her boyfriend at the time, are as follows.

Jason picked Karen up at her home at approximately six P.M. Neither of Karen's parents was present; they were visiting a relative in Laramie. The kids left the house to attend a seven o'clock showing at the Rest Theater in downtown Timber. The movie was *The Blind Mirror,* and the young man taking tickets at the door, Ray Bower, was later able to verify that Jason and Karen did indeed see the movie. Although it was an unusually busy night, Ray remembered them well because Jason had gone out of his way to ridicule Ray's haircut. After the show, which ended at nine o'clock, Jason and Karen rode up to Castle Park. It was Karen's idea, according to Jason. She wanted to see Crystal Falls in the moonlight. They parked in the H lot not far from Snake Tail River and began to hike up along the Pathfinders Trail to the falls. During the hour it took them to reach the top of the falls, they saw nobody. Once at the top, they "hung out," doing nothing in particular.

Near midnight, Jason's attention was drawn by a "strange sound" coming from the other side of a mound of granite that juts up not far from the waterfall. To Jason, the sound was reminiscent of a bear on the prowl. Telling Karen to remain where she was, he went to investigate. He was no sooner on the other side of the mound than he heard Karen scream. Immediately he ran back to where he had left her.

He was greeted with a horrible sight. A large bear was on top of Karen, mauling her as she lay helpless on the ground. Jason reached for a stick and began to beat the animal from behind,

2

trying to force its attention away from Karen. To an extent, he was successful. The bear turned away from Karen long enough to smack him in the face with a paw. He was thrown to the ground where he "remembers" striking his head on a rock and blacking out.

When Jason came to, Karen was dead. Her body had been ravaged beyond recognition. At first, he tried to carry her back down the trail, but because of the seriousness of his own injuries—a swollen left eye and a bruised skull—he had to abandon the idea. He went on alone, and somehow managed to reach his car and drive to the police station in Timber.

At this point our source of information switches to Lt. James Baker, who had just completed his shift and was returning to the station to check out for the day. It was Lieutenant Baker who first heard Jason's account of the death. The officer later described Jason as being in a very agitated state. After listening to his story, the lieutenant quickly headed for Castle Park. Because of dizziness caused by his wounds, Jason was unable to accompany Baker. But he was able to describe specifically where the bear attack had taken place, and where Karen's body lay. Jason was taken to Timber Memorial by a night clerk, where he was examined by Dr. Harry Free. A neurological examination and X-rays showed evidence of a mild concussion. Jason was treated for this condition, and for slight scalp abrasions, and was released to the care of his parents.

Lieutenant Baker reached the top of Crystal Falls at precisely two-thirty. Although he searched the spot Jason had described, he was unable to find Karen's body. He did, however, discover evidence of a struggle. There was a significant amount of blood staining the ground, so much, in fact, that he had no doubt someone had died that night.

At three-thirty the lieutenant was joined by Deputy Jeff Pierce, a part-time employee of the Timber Police Department. Together they continued the search of the area, with no success. It was only when they had taken the trail back down the mountain, and were walking along Snake Tail River, in the vicinity of parking lot H, that they found Karen's body. She was lying in the rushing current, held in place by a large branch that had fallen across the edge of the river. She was, in Baker's words, "a mess."

An autopsy was performed the next day by Dr. Gregory Adams, a coroner out of Cheyenne. His initial findings were made public the following day. To quote: "Karen Holly's rib cage was shattered across the entire right side. Her head had suffered from what appeared to be an extremely powerful blow—the top of the skull was cracked in several places. Whether she died from the former or the latter wound is difficult to say, and of only academic importance. Either injury was sufficiently severe to terminate her life. The blood loss alone from her numerous lacerations would have been enough to kill her."

Dr. Adams concludes by saying Karen Holly had "probably" been the victim of a wild animal attack. The doctor does not offer the type of animal.

I would like to ask the reader to forgive my rehashing the details that have already been adequately reported in these pages on the days following the death of Karen. But I feel it necessary to have the events fresh in your mind before I present new facts that have recently come to light, and before I offer an analysis of the implausibilities in Jason Whitfield's account.

I caught up with Dr. Adams in Cheyenne two days ago. This took some doing, for he is a very busy man, or rather, I must assume he is. In the last three weeks he hasn't had time to return a single one of my calls. When we finally met, I can't say he appeared eager to satisfy my curiosity. He did, however, reveal a couple of interesting details that had come out during Karen's autopsy and that had not been previously released to the press. The first was the discovery of small amounts of human skin under the girl's fingernails. The second concerned the nature of the scratches covering her body; they didn't resemble those normally found on the victim of a grizzly attack. Indeed, it was this point, the coroner confessed, that had made him reluctant to specify that the culprit had been a grizzly. On the other hand, he was quick to assure me it must have been a bear. No other animal would have had the strength to do what had been done to Karen. But when I asked if a person, say a young man with a sledgehammer and a rake of some type, could have inflicted such damage to Karen's body, the doctor would not rule out the possibility.

That surprised me. With all the sophisticated forensic tests that can be done these days, I had assumed a coroner could tell the difference between a murdering bear and a murdering human. If nothing else, I figured a bear would leave quite a few bear hairs lying around. I told the doctor as much. It was then the gentleman suddenly had another appointment to keep. As he was walking away, I called, "Would a grizzly first kill a person, leave the area, and then return and drag the body three hundred yards to a river and throw it in?" The coroner must not have heard my question. He did not answer.

The experts say it was a bear. Jason Whitfield says it was a bear. So what's my problem? And why am I spoiling your breakfast going on about an incident you would all rather forget? Frankly, I'm not sure. It's just that there's something scary about experts who don't want to talk and an eighteen-year-old boy who may have talked too much. It was Karen's idea to hike up to the top of the waterfall, Jason reports. Karen's sister says Karen hated exercise of any type. Then Jason says he heard a strange sound, and thought it might have been a bear, and went to investigate, leaving his girlfriend all alone and unprotected.

Now I don't know Jason personally, but he must be either very brave or very stupid. Why didn't he simply grab Karen's hand and get the hell out of there? Plus, there is the manner in which the grizzly treated Jason. From the sound of things, the boy got off awfully light, especially when you consider that this was a kid who was beating the blasted beast with a club. When I spoke to the doctor who had treated Jason that night, he told me that boy must be one of the luckiest people in the world. He also answered affirmatively when I inquired if it was possible that Jason's wounds were self-inflicted.

I'll leave you with a few more points to ponder. The police will neither confirm nor deny something as basic as whether or not there were grizzly tracks in the vicinity of the incident. A hunt was made for a grizzly, but it was conducted by a few men and lasted only three days. As far as I know, no one has compared the skin under Karen's nails with Jason's skin.

Jason is scheduled to appear next Monday at a preliminary hearing in Cheyenne. This hearing is to determine whether he should be tried in connection with the death of Karen Holly. I have it on good sources the hearing is only a formality, that the state is already prepared to drop the case. As we all know, Carl Whitfield, Jason's father, is mayor of Timber.

Do I believe Jason killed Karen? I'll say again, I don't know. I'll go so far as to say I think the chances are against it. I prefer to think this way because the alternative makes me feel sick.

But maybe this is the reason so little is going on to solve this mystery. None of us even wants to consider this alternative. Maybe we should. Odds were that Karen Holly would have been Timber High's homecoming queen this year. She was only seventeen.

Cindy refolded the paper and tucked it under her arm. She was familiar with this reporter and the slant of the article had not surprised her. Kent Cooke was the small-time investigator type who was always looking for the big conspiracy. He was fanatically liberal, always lashing out at the local government, the police department, authority in general. For years he had been carrying on a personal vendetta with Mayor Carl

Whitfield, who was doubly hexed in Mr. Cooke's eyes, not only because he was in a position of power, but because he was rich.

Cindy was also familiar with the Whitfields' wealth. She saw signs of it every time she went out on a date. She was Jason Whitfield's new girlfriend.

But I am not Karen's replacement.

The article was dumb. A rake and a sledgehammer? Wouldn't Karen have noticed those little niceties as they hiked up to the top of the waterfall? "Hey, Jason, what are you doing with that far-out hammer?" "Just going to crack some rocks, babe." Then there was that point about why the bear hadn't hurt Jason worse when everyone knew a grizzly usually let you alone if you lay perfectly still, which Jason, being unconscious, would have been doing. Finally there was that feeble attempt to create a mystery about the absence of bear tracks. Kent Cooke must have known the area near the waterfall was more rock than dirt, and that it had rained heavily right after Karen had been attacked. Chances were the tracks had been washed away. It was pretty shabby reporting not to mention that tiny detail. No, Kent Cooke wouldn't be getting a Pulitzer prize for this piece. He would probably be getting sued.

You'd deserve it. You ruined my breakfast. And I've already eaten.

Cindy had not known Karen well. Cindy's best friend, Pam Alta, had been Karen's cousin, and the two cousins had not gotten along. Consequently, it had been impossible for Cindy to talk to Karen in a normal way after having listened to Pam tell her what a self-centered weasel her cousin was. Of course, Pam sure felt awful when Karen had died.

Karen had been beautiful, a striking redhead. And

despite Pam's words to the contrary, she had not seemed a bad sort. Certainly, she had been popular. Her boyfriend had, after all, been the best-looking guy in the school. The reporter had gotten one point right. Karen probably would have been homecoming queen.

Cindy turned toward the south. Crystal Falls was just visible between the trees, five miles away—one of those miles being straight up—its early-autumn waters fanning a white veil over the hard brownish-gray cliffs of Castle Park. As she watched, Cindy saw a drifting cloud hug the mountain, and the place where Karen had come to her horrible end was covered in mist. The symbolic quality of the scene, taking place as it did moments after the reporter's dark questions, did not sit well with Cindy.

Jason loved Karen. You just had to listen to his voice when he talked about her to know that.

"Wolf," Cindy called to her big silver dog who had suddenly appeared from the side of the house. He was one dog who fully deserved his name. Wolf had so small a percentage of *real* dog in him that Cindy had had the worst time getting him shots and a license. He was really a civilized monster. It was only when he heard the word *sic*—spoken by her lips and no other's —that his wild heritage emerged. Then he went for the throat. Having him around made her feel sort of invincible.

Wolf licked her right hand, his warm tongue making her realize how cold her fingers had become. She had meant to dash outside, collect the paper, and hurry back in to make her brother breakfast. Alex was probably wondering what had become of her. It wouldn't be good to tell him about the article. As it was, he was not crazy about Jason.

"You wouldn't have any trouble handling a grizzly, would ya, sweetie?" Cindy asked, petting an appreciative Wolf on the head before she turned back toward the house. Wolf followed at her feet, and as she opened the front door, he hurried inside.

Alex was in the kitchen beside the toaster. He was making his own single-course breakfast with a loaf of brown bread and a cube of butter. She gave a disapproving look. Their parents owned a hardware store in downtown Timber and had to be up early and out of the house. As a result, Cindy was accustomed to preparing Alex's breakfast, a task she didn't mind. She enjoyed cooking and usually felt good about doing her younger brother a favor in the morning, since usually he had helped her the previous night with her homework.

"Wouldn't you rather have an omelet or some bacon?" she asked.

"Don't bother," Alex said, retrieving a couple of slices of bread from the toaster and reaching for the knife.

"It's no bother. I meant to have something fixed already."

Alex began to dig into the butter. "You're forgetting what day it is."

"Oh, yeah, race day." Her brother ran cross country for Timber High. Although only a junior, he was the best—or the second best, depending on whether he had a good day or not—runner in the school. He took his sport seriously. On race days he ate only complex carbohydrates for breakfast; in this case, about eight slices of whole grain bread. He wouldn't be eating lunch that afternoon. He skipped the meal because he said there wasn't enough time to digest the food before he had to run. Cindy knew it was because he got so tense immediately before a race that he'd throw up if he had anything in his stomach. "Why don't you at least have a glass of milk with it?" she asked.

"Milk's mucous forming. It could affect my wind."

"Would an apple affect your wind?" She was keen on balanced diets.

"It would if I tried to run with it in my mouth," Alex replied, biting into his toast, glancing out the window. "Looks like a pretty day."

"That's what I thought," she muttered, grabbing a carton of milk off the table and pouring some into a bowl for Wolf, who didn't know about balanced diets and who wasn't worried about winning races. Wolf lapped up the milk hungrily.

He wasn't their only weird animal. Alex owned a blind parrot that had to be a hundred years old. Her name was Sybil, and she could recognize a dozen different people by their voices alone and clearly pronounce each of their names. The one thing that annoyed Cindy about Sybil was that she didn't know *her* name.

"Say hello to Cindy, Sybil," Cindy said, tearing pieces off the front page of the paper and feeding the old bird portions of Kent Cooke's article. Looking at the parrot, you'd swear she could see. Her wide-open soulful eyes possessed a keenly penetrating gaze.

"Mornin', Alex," Sybil chirped, enjoying the article more than Cindy had. Sybil would often chew on a piece of junk all day without swallowing it.

"Cindy," she pronounced carefully. "Cindy."

"Mornin', Clyde."

"Who the hell is Clyde?" Cindy wanted to know.

"He's a friend of Bill's," Alex said. "They were up here the other day, talking to Sybil."

"Mornin', Bill," Sybil said.

"Stupid bird," Cindy scowled.

"Mornin', stupid," Sybil said.

11

"I suppose she's getting closer." Cindy sighed. "Finish your toast. I want to get out of here." She threw the remainder of the paper in the garbage.

Alex wanted to drive. He had just gotten his license. To Cindy that meant it was time he started asking girls out. Alex was so shy around girls she was afraid if he didn't start dating soon, he never would. But it wasn't as though she was trying to force him into anything he didn't really want to do himself. Her brother was a great romantic at heart. That was part of his problem; he elevated girls he had a crush on to such stratospheric heights he was unable to ask them out. His current flame was an English girl new to the area. She was in Cindy's psychology class. Her name was Joni Harper. She was rather reserved, *very* pretty. She was also a senior. This chick didn't need elevating.

"I think you should do it today," she said as they rolled away from the house down the winding road into town. Turning the first corner, they had a glorious view of valley open before them. With so much green life all around, it was hard to imagine how anyone, old or young, could have died in Timber.

"You mean, win the race? I intend to."

"No. I think you should ask Joni out. Today."

Alex concentrated on his driving. "I should probably wait. She hardly knows me."

"How many times have you talked to her since school began last week?"

"Seven times."

Boy, he's counting. "Do you think any other guy in school has talked to her that many times?"

"Probably not."

"Then you know her better than anyone. Just ask her out."

"But when I've talked to her, *I've* done all the talking. I hardly know anything about her."

"You know she likes your voice."

"I think I should wait."

"How long do you think a chick who looks like Joni will go before being asked out?"

Alex considered that. Logic worked wonders on him. "How should I approach her?"

"Depends on the situation. You have to be natural. Strike up a conversation. Then just ask her if she'd like to go to the game with you tonight."

"What if she doesn't like football?"

"She won't turn you down because she doesn't like football."

"You think she might turn me down?"

"No. She's new here. She hardly knows anybody. Why would she turn you down?"

Alex shrugged. "Being new to the area doesn't mean she's feeling desperate. Maybe she doesn't like the way I look."

Cindy studied her brother for a moment before answering. He was a shade under six feet, thin but with wide shoulders and a way of moving that made it clear he worked out often. The last quality was perhaps not a virtue. By nature, Alex was very controlled, and it showed in his physique as an overall tightness. Then again, as Joni herself appeared somewhat cautious, she might appreciate the quality.

His face reflected his intelligence. His blue eyes were deep set and his mouth, though usually set in a pondering line, was wide and could break into a warm grin if given sufficient provocation. He had a head of thick brown hair that any half-witted English girl should enjoy running her fingers through.

"*I* like the way you look," she said.

Alex glanced over at her and smiled. "Want to go to the game with me tonight?"

"Yeah. We'll make it a double date. Jason and I, and you and Joni."

"Jason's playing."

"We could all go out together afterward. It's an early game."

Alex paused. "How did Jason ask *you* out?"

Well, he called me up to thank me for the flowers I sent to Karen's funeral and we got to talking and . . .

It sounded worse than it was. He had thanked her for the flowers, but it had been two weeks after the funeral and who said a period of mourning had to last a certain length of time and to hell with those who talked about it behind her back. They hadn't been married, for god's sake.

"I don't remember. See how spontaneous it must have been?"

Alex frowned. "He probably asked you if you wanted to go to a motel."

Cindy paused. "That's not fair," she said coolly.

Alex glanced at her. "I'm sorry."

"Apology accepted." There was a moment of silence. "Want me to ask the girls on the squad if they'll come to the race today?"

She was a member of the song team. Last year, being on the squad had been a big deal, but lately, especially since school had begun, she'd been wondering if she shouldn't hang up her pom-poms. Wiggling her butt in front of the crowds who came to the games no longer appealed to her, and she no longer felt she had much in common with the other girls on the team. Outside of practice, she never talked to them. They were all still into gossiping about their bodies, and their boyfriends' bodies, and what a rush it was when the two of them got nice and close. This didn't

14

mean she wasn't interested in sex; her fantasy life was so disgustingly rich that Pam had several times accurately accused her of blushing while staring off into empty space. It was just that she was dissatisfied with her life as a whole, while her peers didn't seem to be. She was beginning to realize that everything was *not* going to change when she graduated. Unlike Alex, she had no plans to go away to college. She wasn't dumb, but school didn't do a thing for her.

The way her parents were talking lately, they assumed she'd be working full-time in their hardware store. She'd done that all summer. It was going to be news to them, but she had no intention of going back to those fifty-hour weeks. She had quite a bit saved; she figured she'd travel in June. She hoped seeing other places would give her an idea of what she wanted to do with her life. It was a secret hope of hers that a flying saucer would pick her up on some lonely desert road and make her a galactic ambassador. There just didn't seem to be anything in the world that really thrilled her.

Except a pretty face. I still do love them boys.

She was presently wearing her song uniform and knew she could turn a few heads in it. The colors were blue, white, and gold, and complemented her tan skin and light blond hair nicely. The skirt was cut short, which allowed her to flaunt her long legs and shapely hips. She had a nice figure—she could admit it to herself without having to be an egomaniac—and her face wasn't bad, either. Her eyes were a deep blue and she shared Alex's clearly defined chin, which was the current ideal for beauty in Hollywood. Jason had once told her she looked like the girl next door. The compliment fit. She was the wholesome type.

"I don't want those phonies there," Alex said.

"Why not? They should be there to support you guys."

"If they wanted to support us, they wouldn't have to be reminded that there's a meet today."

"Suit yourself." Alex had his pride. "What about Joni?"

"I'll think about it."

"Great." Cindy decided if he hadn't asked her out by psychology class, she would invite Joni to the race.

CHAPTER

II

ALEX JONES'S PHYSICS CLASS was small. He was the only one in it. Biology was usually enough for the students at tiny—five hundred students during a good year—Timber High. A few hardy minds would go so far as to take chemistry, and this year Chem A had eight people in it. But *physics*—there was a limit to how much preparation an adolescent should have to make for college; at least, that was how Alex's contemporaries saw it. But to Alex, the class wasn't even an elective. He planned on applying to an Ivy League school back East—Yale or Princeton—where he knew the competition would be fierce. He'd need all the preparatory education he could scrape together. Nevertheless, he liked physics and probably would have taken it even if he had planned on working in his parents' hardware store for the rest of his life. He'd always been curious about why the universe worked the way it did. He studied his physics texts alone during fourth period. These, with occasional input from Mr. Magnuson, who taught all the science classes, satisfied many of his questions. But next year he was going to see if he could take an advanced psychology class. There were questions about himself he wasn't finding the answers to in the books he was reading.

Alex didn't know why he worried so much. He didn't know why he felt he had to prove himself. When he looked around, no one was asking him to excel. When he had told his parents he'd asked Mr. Magnuson to set up a special physics program for him, they told him to take a fun class, like sculpture or something, and not put so much pressure on himself. What they didn't realize was that sculpture probably would've been more of a headache. His GPA was a big concern to him, and in art and stuff like that he couldn't be sure of getting an A no matter how hard he tried. For example, he was already no longer a candidate for valedictorian the next year. As a sophomore, he had been required to take creative writing, and the teacher, an irritable old lady who didn't understand the difference between what appealed to her and what was good, had given him two Cs. That had dragged his average down a few tenths of a point and had practically handed Ray Bower the top spot on a silver platter.

The thought of Ray filled Alex with double layers of anxiety. Ray was on the cross-country team with him and had been running strongly. Last week, during the time trials to see who'd run on varsity during the first meet, Ray had finished only five seconds behind him in a three-mile race. And the guy hadn't even looked that tired, whereas Alex had felt exhausted. This was particularly worrisome to Alex because of what had happened the previous fall. Through the first part of the season, he had beaten Ray repeatedly. Then he had developed a nasty case of shin splints, where the muscles of the inner shin began to tear away from the bone. This was particularly bad because the injury produced no sign of being there, outside of what he felt in his own pain centers. Alex knew that a few guys on the team had thought it was all in his head. He wouldn't have minded their talk so much if they hadn't been partly right. The injury was there, that was a fact, but it had affected him more than it should have. Subconsciously, he had to admit to himself, he had probably used it as an excuse to take pressure off himself. In either case, Ray had ended up being the most valuable runner on the team, even though—as far as the whole year was concerned—Alex had outscored him by a large margin. When the vote was taken, the guys' memories had been short.

Alex was also worried about Ray Bower because Mr. Magnuson was having the biology class in the next room choose lab partners, and at the start of class, Ray had been sitting in the back next to Joni. On top of everything else, Ray was a ladies' man. Recently, he had dumped Pam Alta, Cindy's best friend. He was on the prowl.

If Cindy were here she would tell me to get to Joni first.

Alex closed his book, standing. A lot of chatter was coming from biology. That meant the teacher had finished his formal lecture and was letting the kids pair off. Alex stepped through the small equipment area around which the two science rooms were grouped. Mr. Magnuson was inside, taking a hamster out of a cage.

"Alex," the gentleman greeted him, "how are the laws of thermodynamics coming?"

"They seem to be functioning fine, sir, without the benefit of my understanding."

Mr. Magnuson smiled. A pudgy old guy with unkempt gray sideburns that made him look a shade wild, Alex had incorrectly assumed he wasn't serious about what he taught when they'd first met because he had such a jovial personality. In reality, Magnuson was a genuine scientist. Even in hole-in-the-wall Timber, he performed sophisticated immunological experiments on animals. He, in fact, regularly published the results of these experiments in the most prestigious scientific journals in the country. Once, when Alex had asked what he was hoping to discover with all his research, Magnuson had laughed and said, "The secret of immortality, of course!"

"When I get done here," he said, "we can talk about entropy and maybe plan a few practical experiments for you to perform."

"Fine." Alex nodded. "Are you going to kill the hamster?"

Magnuson tied the squirming ball of fur onto a small Formica table that was inclined at a slight slant toward a narrow groove, which was used to drain off the blood into a two-gallon metal tin. "Sorry to say I am. He's already hemorrhaging inside."

"Why?"

"Because of an injection of AT-Seven, an extremely powerful carcinogen, that I gave him two months ago."

Alex occasionally had trouble reconciling the price these little animals had to pay in order to further man's knowledge of disease. But the autopsies never seemed to bother Mr. Magnuson. "I think I'll excuse myself," Alex said, inching toward the biology class.

Magnuson nodded, picking up a scalpel. "Give some of the newcomers inside help with their microscopes, would you? I probably shouldn't have left when I did. I'll be there in a few minutes."

"That's exactly what I was going to do, sir."

Joni wasn't around when Alex entered the class. He was amazed at how much this minor fact caused him to relax. He wasn't looking forward to asking her out. Actually, he was terrified of the prospect. Yet he felt it was something he had to do. She was quite simply the most fascinating thing he had ever seen in his life. He was ninety percent sure she was going to turn him down.

Ray Bower was sitting alone at a corner lab table. Alex wandered over, trying to look casual. Ray brightened at his approach. It was a source of frequent guilt to Alex that Ray didn't realize how much he bugged him. Ray thought they were great friends.

"Looking forward to busting a lung today?" Ray asked as Alex sat down across from him. This was an example of how the dude could get under your skin. The meet that afternoon was all fun and games for him.

"Should be a cake walk," Alex replied. "Brea's got no one who can keep up a five-minute-a-mile pace."

Of course, Timber had two people who could, and looking at Ray, Alex wondered how the guy did it. Ray was on the short side, stout. With his chubby face and long brown hair, he didn't look like an athlete.

"Don't fool yourself." Ray smiled. "I'm going to be on your ass the whole way. Till I pass you at the end, that is."

Alex shrugged. "I always like a good race." He glanced around. "Where's your lab partner?"

"She had to go to her locker."

"She?"

"Joni Harper. You know her."

Damn. Damn. Damn.

"Oh, yeah, Joni. Nice-looking girl."

"Tell me about it. I'm in love with her. You think I should ask her out?"

"Let her get to know you first," Alex muttered,

disgusted. He could see it now, a whole year of watching Ray strolling around campus with one arm around Joni and the other around the cross-country trophy.

"I'd rather she got to know me while we were making out in the front seat of my car."

Alex resisted the impulse to grab a nearby bottle of formaldehyde and throw it in Ray's face. "She's a senior, you know."

Ray nodded. "You're right, I'll have to vacuum out the front seat of my car so she'll know I'm no slouch. Oh, here she comes."

Alex turned his head quickly and swallowed. Seeing her again each time, he always had the irrational fear he would discover she wasn't really as he remembered her. She seemed too perfect. Her figure was sleek, and she walked with a fluid grace, an almost animal deftness, that left him bewildered when he glanced up and saw the delicate lines of her sweet red lips, the pale smoothness of her innocent face. She was like a wild lamb, if there was such a creature. Her hair was long, black, and curly. He had stared into her eyes a half-dozen times and still wasn't sure what color they were, only that they were dark.

"Joni, hi," he said stiffly. She nodded and slid into the chair beside Ray, placing a notebook she had been carrying on the countertop. Her long-sleeved green dress looked expensive; it was clasped at the neck with a silver broach of a bird in flight. "How are you today?" he asked.

"Obviously, she's in excellent form." Ray grinned. "Joni and I are going to have a great time this year, aren't we?"

She smiled faintly. "I think so." Her voice, in spite of its soft accent, sounded a bit hoarse. Indeed, each time he had spoken to Joni, he had thought her voice strained, as if she had recently exhausted it singing or something.

"This class can be a lot of fun," Alex said.

"Biology always is," Ray agreed heartily, his sexual innuendo going right by Joni.

"Are you going to be coming into our class regularly, Alex?" she asked.

"I'm supposed to be learning physics during this time." He added awkwardly, "But I'll probably be stopping in on occasion."

"We'll be lucky if he does," Ray said. "Alex's a genius with the kind of stuff we'll be studying."

Ray was being sincere. Had the positions been reversed, Alex wouldn't have wanted Ray stopping in.

Joni's gaze had strayed to the equipment room. "What is our teacher doing in there?"

Magnuson generally didn't reveal the details of his experiments to his average student. "You don't want to know," Alex said.

"He's disemboweling some poor little rabbit, isn't he?" Ray asked with his usual measure of tact.

"Nah," Alex said.

"But I smell blood," Joni said, still eyeing the center room.

Ray stood. "There's only one way to solve this horrible mystery. Let's go see."

"Ray, I really don't think this is the sort of thing Joni wants to see," Alex said hastily.

"Sure she does. Better she know what a murderer Magnuson is right from the start." He took an unprotesting Joni by the arm as she slid off her stool. Alex didn't know what to do but tag along.

They couldn't have picked a worse time to interrupt Magnuson. He had just sliced the animal lengthwise down the chest, and the blood was still draining off. Alex would have left if there hadn't been the distinct possibility Ray would jokingly shout out what a coward he was.

"Not a pretty sight before lunch, I grant you," the teacher remarked, glancing up, apparently unannoyed at their intrusion.

"God, that's disgusting," Ray said. "Mr. Magnuson, I hate to say it, but there's probably a special hell somewhere for those who were cruel to animals."

"I'll send you a postcard if there is, Bower," Magnuson said, used to Ray's ways.

"If you put all the blood back in," Joni said suddenly, "and sewed the animal together, and had everything just the same as before, it wouldn't get up and walk away, would it?"

"If I could get the hamster to do that, I'd be preparing my Nobel prize speech right now," Magnuson said, taking his hands away from the bloody mess and giving Joni more of his attention. "The main obstacle to bringing about that miracle is the sensitivity of the animal's brain cells. Like our own, they can only survive for a few minutes without oxygen. When you take away the blood, you take away the oxygen."

"But if you could fix each of the brain cells?" Joni asked.

"I still don't think the animal would get up and walk away," Magnuson said wistfully. "Something would still be missing. Some sort of precious ingredient. You could call it life itself."

Joni nodded, apparently satisfied with the explanation.

"I think in that hell for animal murderers there'll be

some cute bunny with a pitchfork that'll keep shoving you back into a boiling pool of black oil," Ray said.

"I didn't know you were a vegetarian, Bower," Magnuson said.

"I'm not," Ray admitted before he realized that meant he was pretty much in the same boat as the teacher. Then all of them laughed, including Joni, at the ridiculousness of a bunny with a pitchfork.

The bell rang a moment later. Class was over. Alex had left his books in the other room, but he was reluctant to leave Joni alone with Ray in case Ray extended her an invitation to go somewhere in his car. Ray was quick to justify Alex's paranoia as they walked back into the biology class.

"Doing anything this afternoon, Joni?" Ray asked.

Joni stared at him a moment. "I don't think so."

Ray smiled. "Great. Come to the cross-country meet. I'll be running. So will Alex. Having you at the finish line will give us a big incentive to hurry and get there."

Joni seemed uncertain. "We'll see."

"You'll be glad you came," Ray reassured her. He punched Alex in the arm. "See you at the tape, buddy."

"I'll be waiting for you," Alex said. Ray thought that was funny. He laughed as he walked away.

Joni collected her books slowly. She appeared lost in thought. Alex didn't know if it was about the invitation she'd just been extended. He glanced around. The class had emptied quickly, and Magnuson was still in the equipment room with the hamster. Alex was alone with Joni. If he was going to ask her out, he'd have no better opportunity.

"I hope the blood didn't bother you," he said. "I would never have taken you in there."

Joni glanced up. "I should go."

"OK," he muttered, trying to remember the things Cindy had told him that morning in the car. Naturalness, spontaneity—

"Do you like football g-games?" he stammered.

"Do you play football, too?"

"No."

"I didn't think so," she replied with a slight frown, turning to leave.

"Wait. Joni?"

She paused and faced him, watching, waiting. Her eyes were black, he could see that now. And they had tiny flecks of purple in them. Or maybe those were green flecks. They were such pretty eyes. "Yes?" she said.

"I was just wondering, you know, if you'd like to go?"

"I don't think so."

Alex nodded weakly. "I was just wondering," he repeated. He should never have listened to his sister. He should have listened to his intuition, which had been telling him all along he would be lonely all his life.

Joni suddenly set down her books and reached out and touched his left shoulder. The feel of her hand on him sent all kinds of strange currents going in his body. "You're nice," she said seriously.

He forced a chuckle. "I think you're nice, too. But if you don't want to go, it's fine, you know. What I mean is, it's no big deal."

She squeezed the top of his arm before letting go. "I'll come to the race," she said.

"Huh?"

26

"I'll watch you run," she said. "I'd rather do that."

Then she picked up her books and walked away.

I'd better win, Alex thought. He didn't know whether to celebrate or not. In the end, he just worried some more.

CHAPTER
III

CINDY JONES AND Pam Alta were sitting in their favorite spot at their favorite time of day. Set in the northwest corner of Timber High's courtyard was a tree stump from a pine that must have once been the pride of the valley; the thick knob of wood was easily six feet across. What made the stump especially appealing to Cindy and Pam, and which kept practically everyone else away from it, was the fact that the tree had been felled six feet above the ground. Neither of the girls was afraid of heights. They loved the view from their perch, especially at lunchtime, when they could sit and swing their legs in the sun and watch the entire student body bustling beneath them.

At present, Pam was doing more talking than watching. She was raving about Bala, a foreign exchange student from Kenya. In America for the school year, he was staying at Pam's house. From their Olympian vantage point, they could see Bala standing to the side of the snack-bar line, apparently searching for somebody. Cindy thought he looked like the direct descendent of an exotic African king. Pam was already in love with him.

"He's so polite," Pam said. "He says 'please' and 'thank you' when you ask him what's new. Last night at the dinner table, when I finished my milk, he immediately jumped up and got the carton from the frig, just in case I wanted some more. I hadn't even said I wanted more. You know, Cindy, how I only drink milk 'cause of all those doctors on Donahue talking about calcium deficiencies and your bones falling apart when you turn thirty. I really can't stand the stuff. So what could I do? Here he's flown halfway around the world to serve me milk, and I don't want any more? Nah, I just couldn't turn him down. I ended up polishing off another couple of glasses."

"Bad for your wind," Cindy muttered, spooning down a cup of strawberry yogurt.

"What?"

"Nothing."

Pam stopped and thought a moment. "You know what's bothering me about this whole relationship?"

"That it doesn't really exist?"

"No. That it's kind of incestuous."

"Bala's visiting for a while. He's not your brother." Cindy laughed when she thought about it some more. "God, he's six and a half feet tall. You look like someone stepped on you. And he's—he's *black*. How could you even imagine you were related?"

Pam was reassured. "So you think I should make a pass at him?"

Cindy raised an interested eyebrow. Pam was no one's choice for Miss Timber. She looked too much like her old boyfriend, Ray Bower. She was a head shorter than Cindy and her backside was chunky. She also had a big nose. Yet Pam somehow avoided being a dog, and Cindy thought it was because she always seemed so ready for a good time. She was not all talk, not when it came to sex. Every time she'd been alone with Ray, Cindy had received a full report. It was no wonder Alex was having trouble beating Ray if half the stories Pam said were true. The guy had endurance.

Cindy was still a virgin. Pam thought the condition was akin to having bad acne. Cindy was in no special hurry. Not this very minute, anyway.

"I don't see why you shouldn't make one," Cindy said.

"I don't know. My mother's sort of old-fashioned. She thought *Guess Who's Coming to Dinner* was a horror film. But it would be neat to walk around campus with him holding my hand. Then hopefully Ray would see what a woman of international appeal he'd given up."

Cindy noted Pam's choice of words—*"he'd given up."* Initially, Pam had tried to lead people to believe she'd dumped Ray, and not vice versa. For a few weeks there, happy-go-lucky Pam had been one miserable dog. Only Cindy knew how much she still wanted him back.

"Your mom's not prejudiced," Cindy said. "After all, she did invite Bala to stay at your house."

Pam snickered. "There's a big difference in her mind between sharing her house and sharing her daughter."

"I suppose."

Pam changed the subject. "Have you seen Jason today?"

Cindy felt a stab of uneasiness. "No. Have you?"

Pam nodded. "He's breathing fire."

"That damn article. You read it, too?"

"The whole school read it."

"It's just a bunch of crap," Cindy said defensively. "Kent Cooke's only using Jason to get at Mr. Whitfield. You didn't believe any of it, did you?"

"I believe the part where Karen died."

"Pam!"

"All right, don't get excited. No, I didn't believe that Jason suddenly developed a grizzly's strength and tore Karen apart. Or that he had a sledgehammer hiding in the bushes. None of the other kids does, either. But Cooke makes one point I think most of the school *does* believe. Jason's not being totally up front about everything that went down that night."

"Be specific," Cindy said in an even tone.

"I can't be," Pam said, looking genuinely puzzled. "But he took her up there at night. You'd think he could've looked after her better."

This was a familiar point of view. In the days following the funeral, Cindy had heard it discussed in bits and snatches by the townsfolk when she'd been working at her parents' hardware store. Since, at the time, she hadn't been going out with Jason, she hadn't given the talk much heed. But even then it had struck her as unfair. The end result was that he was seen as a coward. Why hadn't he done something, for god's sake? People would gossip to one another. He was *the man,* after all. Of course, they never said what he could have done.

"Swell," Cindy muttered. "You pick any guy in the school and put him in a cage with you and a grizzly and we'll see how well he protects you. I bet you wouldn't even find a guy who'd have the guts to try to hit the bear with a stick."

"Exactly. None of us think Jason hit his grizzly with a stick. The common consensus is he took one look at the beast and put his ass in gear. That's what I would have done."

"Then how can you accuse Jason of being a coward?"

"'Cause I'm a coward, myself. Look, don't get all

31

bent out of shape. I'm just telling you what people are saying. I still think Jason's a babe, and I think you should try to make him a happy man one of these nights soon." She added, "What are you guys doing tonight after the game?"

"I don't know. We might be going out with Alex and Joni Harper." She hadn't seen Alex since they'd parted in the parking lot that morning, although she had searched for him at the beginning of lunch. There was a lot of stuff they'd done in Algebra II that wasn't clicking. Her brother was always so much better at explaining things than her math teacher. He had a lot more patience. And she'd wanted to see if he really had asked Joni out. Despite what she'd said in the car, she was worried Joni might turn him down. But she hadn't been able to find him. He often went for a walk at lunch on race days.

"Alex asked Joni out?" Pam said. "That's great. That's absolutely wonderful. I'm happy for him. She's a doll."

Cindy looked at her suspiciously. Her enthusiasm was out of place, even though Pam really did like Alex. Last year, she had gone to every one of the cross-country races and shouted her support for him instead of Ray, despite the fact Ray was her boyfriend at the time. Her kind remark about Joni was what lacked sincerity. Ray had broken up with her not long after Joni had appeared in town, and Pam had insinuated several times that Joni was partly responsible. This appeared to be nothing but pure paranoia.

Before she could respond to Pam's comment, she noticed Bala walking away from the snack bar in the company of Joni. Apparently, Joni was the one he had been waiting for. Watching them together, Cindy was strangely affected. Her mind started to draw a connec-

32

tion her eyes could not support. Bala was a powerfully built black. Joni was a trim fair-skinned girl. Yet in some way, they looked the same to her, somehow closely related. The impression seemed to emerge from the way they moved. Cindy couldn't pinpoint it any closer than that. Indeed, a moment later, she was wondering what had caused her to find a similarity at all. They were both new, she told herself, that's what they had in common. That was all. Bala's walk was completely different from Joni's. She had to take two steps to his one.

"I didn't know Bala knew Joni," Cindy said.

"He was here only a couple of days when they met. I got the impression Joni wasn't crazy about him. Bala was going too far out of the way to be nice to her—even by his standards. And that's saying a lot."

"How did they meet?" Cindy asked. Bala was smiling, talking freely. Joni was chewing on an apple, nodding occasionally.

"I don't remember. Maybe Karen brought her over. Karen and Joni were pretty good friends."

"Really? How did that get started?"

"They lived next door to each other. I think Karen sought her out. Once she saw how beautiful Joni was, I think she figured she'd better get on her good side. But then Karen seemed to end up really liking her."

Pam's observation about Joni's lack of interest in Bala appeared correct. Already, Joni seemed to be trying to break off her conversation with him. A moment later she did so, walking away with her apple, leaving Bala staring at her back.

"Let's go talk to him," Cindy said, collecting her lunch bag.

"Bala? Why?"

"Because I want to, that's why."

33

They climbed down from the tall stump and headed through the mass of loitering students. Cindy could feel her pulse quickening. This wouldn't be the first time she had spoken to Bala. They had talked on several occasions during the last few weeks, usually when she was visiting Pam at her house. She'd been doing more of that lately, going over to see Pam, or maybe Bala himself, if she wanted to be entirely honest with herself. He held a totally new attraction for her. A minute ago she had compared him in her mind to a king. There was something noble in his demeanor. Yet his real allure for her was something more abstract, something she had yet to figure out. He seemed more than human, as if he were surrounded by a magnetic aura.

Pam had no idea Cindy felt this way. And it wasn't as though it would ever go anywhere. Jason was her boyfriend and he was the mayor's son and Bala was just a beautiful body passing through on his way back to Africa.

I'm so superficial.

Bala greeted them with a bright smile. "Good afternoon, girls," he said in his deep voice, a velvety concoction of back bush accent and impeccable British English. She briefly wondered if the accent similarities had triggered her association between him and Joni.

"Hello, Bala." Pam smiled. "Cindy wants to ask you something."

"Yes, Cindy?"

Talking to Bala, she always had to incline her head toward the heavens. This didn't add to her confidence around him. "Yeah," she muttered, "I wanted to ask if you had—ah, a last name. And how you spell it?" Pam was always pulling pranks like this on her.

"I have several last names. One relates to the tribe I

am part of. We are called the Mau Dogan. Another is what you would call my family name. It is Retala."

"So your full name is Mr. Bala Mau Dogan Retala?" Pam said.

Bala smiled. "Bairavee Bala Retala of Mau Dogan is closer."

"Where's the Bairavee come from?" Cindy asked.

Bala hesitated a moment before answering. "I am directly descended from a shaman, or what you might know as a sorcerer. My grandfather is considered a mighty shaman. As a show of respect for him, my people call him Bairavee. This can't be translated directly into English. It means approximately "he who gathers the soul." Because we are related, I am also sometimes called Bairavee."

"I'll just call you Bala," Pam said. "But you better write down all those names for Cindy 'cause she is *so* curious about how they're spelled."

Bala looked doubtful. "Is this important to you, Cindy?"

"You don't have to bother," Cindy said, intrigued with his reference to shamanism.

"It is no bother at all," Bala said, taking a pencil from his back pocket, searching for something to write on. "In my fascination with all aspects of your lives, I forget my cultural background must be as intriguing to you."

"Everything must be completely different for you," Cindy said, handing him a scrap of paper torn from her lunch bag. His command of their language never ceased to amaze her. It was as though he had been born to it. "Don't you feel homesick?"

"In many ways, I feel more at home in your country than in mine. You do not realize how fortunate you are. Reason predominates here. People do not decide what they are going to do next because of the ways the birds arranged the leaves on the ground in the morning. My tribe is sunk in superstition. I have rebelled against it all my life."

"Is that why you were chosen to be a foreign exchange student?" Cindy asked.

The question seemed to catch Bala off guard. He didn't answer immediately, and then they were interrupted by Jason. The timing was unfortunate. It looked like she had just asked Bala for his phone number. Jason apparently saw it that way.

"Hey, what's going on here?" he asked, trying to sound only mildly interested, unable to hide the edge in his voice.

"We're picking names for Christmas gifts," Pam said. "Cindy's got to get Bala something."

"Jason, you know Bala, don't you?" Cindy said quickly. "Bala this is my—friend, Jason Whitfield."

Friend, not boyfriend. What am I thinking?

"Pleased to meet you," Bala said, extending his hand. Jason was six feet tall and no sissy, but his fingers almost disappeared in Bala's grip.

"Yeah, I've seen you around," Jason said. He turned to Cindy. "But where have you been? I've been looking all over for you."

"She's been with me," Pam said.

Jason glanced at his watch. It was Swiss, and if he was ever down on his luck and had to hock it, he would have food to eat for a long time. "The bell's going to ring in a few minutes," he said. "Let's go out to the parking lot. I want to talk."

"I'll see you both in psychology," Cindy called over her shoulder as she hurried to catch up with Jason, who was already walking away. There was no doubt about it, he was in a foul mood.

They didn't speak until they were out in the lot and

standing next to Jason's new motorbike. It was a
Honda 1000 and he'd once gotten it up to a hundred
with her on the back, and she hadn't spoken to him
for two days. He only purchased the cycle after Karen
had died. He always drove like a nut, which worried
her. It was as though he were trying to show people he
wasn't scared of anything.

"I read it," she said, deciding to get right to the
problem. "It was so unfair."

Jason sucked in a breath and Cindy braced herself
for an abusive tirade directed at Kent Cooke and
possibly the rest of Timber. But he held his breath a
moment and then let it out slowly, turning in the
direction of Castle Park. The waterfall wasn't visible
but she imagined he could see it, anyway, in his
memory, running with red waters. He sighed, now
looking more sad than bitter. She wanted to hug and
comfort him but hesitated for reasons that were
themselves unfair. His sorrow looked somehow
incongruous on his black-haired, gray-eyed movie
star face. Jason was the kid who'd had everything:
the best-looking girl in the school, a forty-grand
sports car, and a carefree future fat with daddy's
money. But now he had lost the respect of his
peers, and that he couldn't buy back. And he knew
it.

"Thank you," he said finally. "I think those were
the first kind words I've heard all day."

"Aren't the guys on the team rallying around you?"
Jason was the school's starting fullback. He was pretty
good.

"Yes and no," he said, looking at her. "They'll
come up and say something supportive and then
they'll have to add a little joke about bears or bumps
on the head. You know what bugs me the most about
that article? It was the phony pain that jerk tried to

make you think he felt over Karen's death. But he didn't know her. He didn't feel a damn thing when he heard she was dead, except the satisfaction Carl Whitfield's son was involved."

She put an arm around his shoulders. "After the hearing next Monday, when the facts are reviewed by the court, everyone will see you did everything you could."

"I wished I believed that," he said, shaking his head. "No, I think something's got to be done."

"There's nothing you can do. You did all you could that night. You've got to get on with your life."

He stared at her for a moment. "Let's go up there tonight."

"Where? Up to the top of the falls?"

"Yeah, after the game. It'll still be early."

"But—why?"

"I haven't been up there since Karen died. I need to go. I need to get something out of my system. Will you come with me?"

"But my brother was going to ask this girl out. I thought maybe we could do something with them. He's never gone out with a girl before, and I think he could use the moral support."

"We could bring him and his date along."

"You wouldn't mind?"

"No, I always like having Alex around. He's a good kid."

Cindy considered a moment. "Do you think it would be safe?"

"The chances of the grizzly still being around is about one in ten thousand. Will you come?"

The area around the top of the waterfall had always been one of her favorite places. But like Jason, she had stayed away from there since Karen had died. Psychologically, for him especially, there might be a value in returning to the spot. It would be like confronting the problem head on, she reasoned.

"Sure, I'll go with you. And if you want just the two of us to go, that would be OK. Alex might want to be alone with the girl, anyway."

Jason leaned over and gave her a quick kiss. "Thanks. You're the only friend I have. But invite your brother. I want him there. Who's his girl?"

"Well, she's not really his yet. But he's working on it. Her name's Joni Harper. Do you know her?"

"I've seen her."

"She's pretty, isn't she?"

"Not next to you," he said, kissing her again on the cheek, before throwing his leg over his motorcycle. He gunned the engine. In the distance, she could hear the bell ringing, signaling the end of lunch.

"Are you ditching?" she asked.

"Yeah, got some stuff I've got to take care of."

"What?"

"Just some stuff."

"That's too bad. I was hoping you could come to Alex's race after school."

Jason showed interest. "Ray Bower's running against him, isn't he?"

"Yeah."

Jason gunned the engine again, his eyes cold. "Tell Alex for me I hope he kicks Ray's ass. You know how the article said Ray remembered me 'cause I ridiculed his haircut? That really pissed me off. I've known Ray since we were ten years old. And that night, I didn't say a blessed thing about his haircut. Ray just told Kent Cooke that so the two of them could establish right away in the reader's mind what a violent dude I am." Jason shook his head. "Ray's got some real bad luck coming to him."

"He's just got a weird sense of humor. He went with

Pam for too long." She patted him on the back, trying to sound cheery. "If I don't see you before the game tonight, score five touchdowns for me."

He nodded grimly. "I think tonight's going to be a good night."

She waved as he drove away, still curious about where he was going. Jason never ditched.

Miss Clemens taught psychology. She was young, had large breasts, and often bent over in her short skirts. All the boys liked her, and most of the girls, including Cindy, who had observed with an appreciative eye all the times Miss Clemens had counseled the kids that were going through rough times.

Cindy arrived at class a few minutes late and took a seat across from Joni, who didn't turn to acknowledge her. Cindy took that as a sign Alex hadn't asked her out. It seemed to her most girls would give some reaction to the sister of a guy who had just approached them.

Miss Clemens was apparently introducing Bala as a speaker. She wanted him to discuss how daily life in his village differed from life in Timber. Cindy thought this a fortunate coincidence. She could finish the conversation she'd started at lunch without fear Pam would try to embarrass her.

"Unless you have something in particular you'd like to begin with," Miss Clemens said, sitting behind her desk, which always frustrated the guys' view of her fine legs, "you could start by accepting questions."

She was trying to relax Bala, which was obviously unnecessary. He sat up front on a stool, and it was as if, without speaking, he already had command of the room. His size alone wasn't responsible for creating the effect, Cindy thought. There was something else.

Bairavee Bala.

"I would appreciate any question," he said softly. Pam immediately raised her hand. Bala smiled. "Yes, Pam?"

"Do all the guys in your village look like you?"

"We are all black," he replied with a straight face. The room broke up. Bala smiled again. Another hand was raised. "Could you tell us exactly where your village is in relationship to Kenya's big cities, how many people it holds, and what degree of Western influence you guys get?" a fellow named Ken asked.

"Those are good questions. Mau Dogan is sixty miles west of Nairobi, the capital of the country. Until ten years ago, our population was close to two thousand. But with the famine we've been having, we're down to less than half that. Our main source of Western influence has been a doctor and his wife. His name was Herbert Stevens and he used to care for the people of our village and those in neighboring villages. It was his wife who taught me how to speak English. Her name was Valerie. I was a favorite of hers. She used to get me tapes and books." He added quietly, "But they don't live in Mau Dogan anymore."

"The drought must have been hard on your people," Miss Clemens said sympathetically. Bala responded in a surprising fashion. His voice took on a stern note.

"It was, but it was largely our fault. We had plenty of water. It was right beneath us. All we had to do was dig wells and develop storage facilities. Do not misunderstand me, not all of Africa could have escaped the effects of the drought so easily. But we could have. We just would not listen to Dr. Stevens and other representatives of UNICEF. We had our 'customs' that said

41

you could anger the soil by digging too deeply into it."

"But these customs must be deeply ingrained in the psyche of your people," Miss Clemens said. "It must be difficult to overcome them."

Bala would have none of this rationalization. "It was more difficult for my people to die," he said.

Cindy raised her hand. Bala nodded in her direction. "Do some of these old-fashioned ideas come from the shaman in your village?" she asked.

Bala hesitated and Cindy recognized why. She had, after all, just asked about his grandfather. "Yes."

"But doesn't this person know things that, say, a Western doctor has no knowledge of?" Cindy asked.

"Maybe," he answered reluctantly.

"You're not sure?" she asked, surprised.

"I am not."

"Could you give us an example of abilities or knowledge your shaman *might* possess that we would consider extraordinary?" She'd always had a deep fascination with things mystical. Alex said it was because she didn't realize how interesting science could be. She thought her interest sprang from the realization of how much scientists didn't know.

Bala scanned the room. He appeared to come to a decision. "Very well. At lunch I told you our shaman is referred to as Bairavee, 'he who gathers the soul.' Our Bairavee has given demonstrations where he has taken a person, a young boy, and put him in a trance by chanting softly in his ear. When the boy was ready, an animal was tied directly in front of him. The choice of animal varied. Sometimes it was a monkey, sometimes it was a snake or a lion. Once even a fish held in a bowl of water was used. Then our Bairavee used an ability people in the West definitely do not have. He put the *animal* in a trance, using a different sort of chant. This was only the beginning. With the boy and animal staring into each other's eyes, our Bairavee—you will have trouble believing this and I can understand how you feel—transferred their spirits. The spirit of the animal went into the boy, and the spirit of the boy went into the animal. The experience of the boy was that he was indeed in the animal. If a lion was being used, he would feel the strength of the lion's claws, even understand what it was like to *think* like a lion. But at all times he never lost the awareness he was still a boy. Therefore, I suppose you could not call it a complete transfer, but a merger of some type. Of course, how the animal felt during these demonstrations, I could not say."

"That's nothing new to us," Pam said. "Merlin was doing that to Arthur centuries ago."

There were a few chuckles, not many. Bala was apparently unaware of the reference. "Pardon?" he said politely.

"Never mind her," Miss Clemens said. "Bala, were there any side effects from these *spirit journeys,* or whatever you want to call them, on the people who went into the animals?"

"The boy did not feel he'd been harmed in any way," Bala said carefully.

"Did he feel he'd grown from the experience?" Cindy asked, not bothering to raise her hand.

"I do not understand," Bala said.

"Did he take away with him a better understanding of what it was like to be the animal he'd just gone into?" she asked.

Bala was beginning to look as if he wished he had never brought up the subject. "To be frank, I cannot say if these experiences were anything more than hallucinations brought on by an elaborate form of hypnosis."

"Do *you* think it was only hypnosis?" she asked.

Bala looked down. "Yes."

The subject was changed. Someone asked for details on the relief efforts being made throughout Africa. Bala answered with more enthusiasm than he had shown for sorcery. Cindy's mind began to wander. She was worried about starving children, but at the moment the topic just didn't fire her imagination. She wondered what it would be like to go into an eagle and soar high above the mountains. One day, she thought, she'd like to meet Bala's grandfather. "Hypnosis" was a convenient word she felt was too often used to explain the inexplicable.

When the bell rang at the end of class, Pam hurried to Bala's side and threw Cindy a look that said she wanted to be alone with him. Maybe she did know, Cindy thought, about a "certain someone's" attraction to him. Oh, well, that was life in relationship lane.

She remembered her self-made promise to invite Joni to the race. The English girl sure could move. Cindy only caught up with her after Joni had made it halfway across the courtyard.

"Joni," she called. The girl slowed and glanced her way. "You remember me, Cindy Jones?"

Joni nodded. "You're Alex's sister." A slight smile touched the corners of her mouth, but her large black eyes remained impassive.

"That's right." No sense beating around the bush. "Did you know Alex has an important race today?"

"Yes. I'll see you there."

"You're coming?"

"Yes."

"Do you know where it is?"

"Yes," Joni said, returning to her original pace.

Cindy slowed to a halt.

"Great," she called.

Joni nodded without turning around.

CHAPTER

IV

*T*HEIR WARM-UP WAS COMPLETE. The race started in less than ten minutes. And Ray Bower was eating a package of Hostess miniature chocolate doughnuts and drinking a carton of milk.

"I need the sugar to fuel my body for the upcoming ordeal," Ray said when Alex warned him he would probably cramp. "Besides, I'm hungry." He offered him a doughnut. "Are you sure you don't want one?"

"I'll pass," Alex said, feeling he might be the one who was getting a cramp. He had a minor stitch in his left side, under his rib cage. But he had to wonder if he didn't usually have a bit of tightness there, that he wasn't simply making an issue of it because this was the first race of the year.

Alex scanned the stadium field for Joni Harper, and didn't see her, feeling as relieved as he did disappointed. He did catch sight of his sister, however, and Pam. They were standing next to the bleachers, not far from where the exhausted junior varsity were finishing. He had no reservations about their presence. Cindy was still wearing her song uniform, naturally; she was required to wear it the whole day before a game. She was the only one from the pep squads who had taken the time to come. That was fine with him. Most of those rah-rah girls had about as much upstairs as a Ping-Pong ball. That was what he liked about Joni. She didn't talk much, but there was obviously a lot going on behind those deep black eyes. He searched again for her.

"Looking for Joni?" Ray asked, stuffing a doughnut in his mouth.

"No."

Ray took a swig of milk, spilling several drops on his gold warm-up jacket. "I wish she was here."

"And what if you run badly?"

"If I do, so what? It won't change a hair on her great body." He crumpled up his doughnut wrapper, showing a trace of disappointment that they were all gone. "Besides, I'm probably going to win."

Alex nodded toward the finish line. "Our JV's sure getting their butts kicked. Brea's stronger this year."

"Nah. They're probably running their varsity now. We'll have no problem." He laughed. "I can't wait to hear Pam screaming for me to trip. I'm glad she's here." He paused. "You know, Alex, I think I'm going to try to get back together with her. I really miss her whining in my ear."

"Then what's all this talk about Joni?"

"Joni's a fantasy. I'm going to ask her out. I'm going to try to get her in the sack. I think it would make my junior year. But I could never have her as a girl-friend."

Alex was curious in spite of the disgust he felt at how casually Ray could talk about having sex with someone he felt he would have been willing to give his life for. "Why not?" he asked.

"She's too different from me. She's too refined. I can't see laying around the house and watching TV with her. Can you?"

"I don't watch much TV," Alex said. "So why even ask her out if you feel this way?"

"I can't help myself. She's cast a spell on me. Just once, I've got to know what that soft white skin feels like under my fingers." He stopped, squinted at him. "As long as that's OK with you, buddy?"

The question caught Alex off balance. Was Ray serious? Of course he was, the blind fool. He would back off if asked. But Alex realized he could never ask. He couldn't admit he was unwilling to compete fairly with Ray in this area any more than he could ask Ray not to race against him to his fullest ability.

"I don't give a damn what you do with your hairy fingers," he said.

Ray smiled. "I'll shave them before our date."

A few minutes later the last of the JV runners staggered in. They had been crushed. Alex took it as a bad sign. Cindy and Pam walked over to give him a last word of encouragement.

"How do you feel?" his sister asked, brushing a hair off his shoulder.

"He's not very hungry, that's for sure," Ray said, finishing his milk.

"I hope you barf those doughnuts up all over yourself at the second mile," Pam told Ray.

"I feel strong," Alex lied.

"Varsity!" the starter, Brea's coach, called. Their own coach was stationed at the midway point, where he would be giving them one of the split times.

"Just do your best," Cindy said seriously, giving him a kiss on the cheek. "That's all you have to do."

"Where's my kiss?" Ray asked Pam, belching.

Pam whacked him on the top of the thigh. "There's a charley horse to slow you down."

"See you in less than fifteen minutes," Alex told Cindy, referring to the time he planned to break, his throat bone dry. He almost wished he could have had a sip of Ray's milk.

They gathered at the starting line, pulling off their sweats. "Ready!" the coach shouted, raising the gun toward the sky. Alex crouched down, taking a deep breath.

"Hey, I forgot to tie my right shoe," Ray said casually.

The gun went off and Alex sprung forward with the crowd. It was a jumbled start, which was often the case at the beginning of the season, with runners bumping into one another. As Alex hurried down the first straightaway of the track, before exiting the stadium, he was distracted by a thin dark-haired girl standing in center field.

Joni.

A Brea runner, a tall blond Alex did not recognize from last year, set the pace. It was fast. Staying with him, Alex could feel the rest of the pack falling back. He didn't know what Ray was doing and wondered if he had stopped to tie his shoe. A quick glance over his shoulder told Alex nothing.

The course was three miles long and it was rough. It led out the rear of the school onto a dirt path that wound through the forest for two miles, following an initial gradual downgrade before slamming into two steep hills. The last mile consisted of a loop around the school, with the finish in the stadium.

As they passed into the shade of the trees, Alex wondered if he wasn't making a mistake. He knew he was going too fast too early. What he didn't know was if the guy he was following was going to burn out or keep up this pace till the end. Because the guy was not familiar, he thought it prudent to stay close in case he was an iron lung new to Brea High. On the other hand, if that were the situation, he probably couldn't beat the guy, anyway, and he would just be setting himself up for his own burn-out, virtually assuring Ray second place.

When they reached the first mile, Alex knew for a fact he had chosen the wrong strategy. The time was four minutes and forty-two seconds. He was eighteen seconds under his pace! Plus the blond-haired dude was already faltering. Alex passed him as the path dipped into a grassy meadow and the sun glared from behind the tree branches. He risked another brief glance over his shoulder, but didn't see Ray. That counted for nothing. With the turns in the path, Ray could be five seconds back and he'd never know it until too late.

With his running companion slipping behind, Alex tried to will himself into his usual rhythm, without much success. He was breathing too hard; he felt as if he had already tackled the hills, and it depressed him to know that they were still to come.

Coach Tyler was waiting at the midpoint with his scratchy voice and ticking stopwatch. "You're looking good, Alex," he called. "Seven-seventeen—seven-eighteen— Looking good."

The man was gone in a blur. That was the trouble with people who were there to support you. They couldn't take away a morsel of fatigue. Coach Tyler always said he was looking good, even when he was dying inside. The time was all that was important. He was still pushing too hard too soon. And, God, did his body know it. Stinging sweat dripped into his eyes. A cramp began to form in his *right* side.

The first hill was upon him a minute later. Leaning forward slightly, he drove with his arms. He wasn't a good hill runner. Ray, with his short legs, was better. Nearing the top, Alex could feel a heavy lactic acid debt accumulating in his shoulders, spreading into his arms. He was literally gasping for air. At least now he would be able to see where he stood. For the third time, he threw a glance behind. But what caught his attention was not the other runners, but a bank of thick black clouds gripping the mountains behind Castle Park. Lightning sparked in their midst and he spotted a hazy band of shadow shifting over the peaks. Rain was falling heavy up there. By tonight, Crystal Falls would be gorged.

Alex shifted his gaze to the path he had just covered. What he saw was not totally unexpected, and yet, he was shocked. Ray was at the foot of the hill. And the blond dude hadn't faded much at all; he was on Ray's shoulder. Alex had at best fifteen seconds on them. That should have been a lot with just over a mile to go. But with the lead in his legs, a minute lead wasn't safe.

Why do I put myself through this?

Joni and Cindy were waiting for him at the finish line, that was why. He plowed forward.

The second hill, shorter and steeper, did not drain him as badly as he'd feared. Indeed, as he emerged from the forest and raced along the sidewalk at the west side of the school, hearing shouts of encouragement from the stadium above, he began to believe he might pull it off. He was still running against steadily increasing fatigue but he suddenly felt more in sync. His wind had settled into a decent rhythm.

The stadium was close at hand but before he could enter it he had to head away from it for a couple of minutes. At the southwest corner of the school, he plunged into the campus proper, racing along a path that had been cleared of traffic by other members of the team. Their shouts mixed with the echoing pounding of his feet. Someone called out that his lead was seventeen seconds.

He was rounding the gym when disaster struck. Two cheerleaders were painting a poster for the night's game directly on top of the gold chalk line that marked the course. Maybe his teammates had forgotten to tell them to move. Maybe the girls had figured the geeks on the cross-country team should run around them. It didn't really matter. He saw them too late. His left foot caught on one girl's arm. His right foot slipped on the drying blue poster paint. He didn't have a chance to brace his fall with his hands. He hit the asphalt hard, his left knee taking the brunt of the impact.

"We're sorry!" one of the redfaced girls cried as he rolled on his belly and tried to get to his feet. He wasn't angry, not yet. His left leg was stinging something awful. A wad of flesh had been scraped away. Blood oozed from the cut. He had to get going.

The fall had an insidious effect on him, but not because of the physical damage it had done or the time it had stolen from his lead. Back in stride, he realized the wound was superficial. It looked nasty but it hadn't weakened his strength. Also, between going down and getting up, he had sacrificed at best five seconds. No, his problem was with the excuse the fall had given him, and the one half of his personality that was always looking for an excuse so he wouldn't have to feel so much pressure. By no means did he intend to quit. He still wanted to win just as badly. The only real difference inside was he began to entertain the thought of saving his strength for the finish. He was nearly exhausted. The cramp in his right side felt like an appendix ready to burst. Suddenly it seemed wiser to play it conservative. Besides, no one would question his slowing down after such a terrible fall. It was really quite simple, as simple and handy as the shin splints had been last year. He slacked his pace a notch.

But you're not hurt! You only have to gut it out for another two minutes! Joni is here!

It was strange how what was surely his stronger side wasn't nearly as persuasive. He eased back some more, taking a welcome breather.

Ray caught and passed him a hundred yards before the stadium, and with him, the tall blond. He watched them go by with a mixture of detachment and despair. Their lead widened as they ran onto the track and began to round toward the finish line. He watched and did nothing till he saw Joni standing beside Cindy and Pam in the center of the football field. Cindy and Pam were bouncing up and down and screaming at the top of their lungs. Joni had her hands clasped behind her back. She was not yelling or moving. And yet, he could feel her eyes on him. He remembered what it had been like to stare into them that morning. Such pretty eyes, watching him lose.

Now, you idiot!

Alex accelerated sharply, a rising panic flushing every trace of fatigue from his limbs and every indecisive thought from his mind. He realized the precariousness of his situation. How could he have squandered a hundred-yard lead! But all was not lost. Ray had thirty yards on him, the blond twenty. Alex had a superb kick. He had half a lap to close the gap.

He almost made it. Had the course been a few yards longer, he would have won. He had burst past the guy from Brea and was close enough to reach out and touch the tape when Ray hit it. He stumbled against Ray's back and slipped around him as they went into the chute. The girl at the end of the flimsy funnel handed him the number one position stick. She probably thought he had won. He took a look at it and broke it in half.

"Nice race, buddy," Ray said, bent over, sweat

pouring off his brow. "Can't believe you finished after going down like that."

"Yeah," Alex croaked, his heart shrieking in his chest. He wanted to congratulate Ray on his outstanding victory. But he didn't know if he could bear the sound of the words.

Ray coughed and straightened. Hands patted him on the back, lines of praise flowing over him. He glanced around with a big smile on his face. "I hope they have another pack of doughnuts in the machine by the snack bar. I'm starving. Hey, Alex, want to go eat somewhere after we shower?"

Alex shook his head and walked away. The entire lower half of his left leg was covered with blood. In the days to come the whole school would probably talk of how Alex Jones rose from the dead to finish the race. What heart. What a man. What a bunch of crap.

"Alex?" Cindy said, hurrying to his side, pain in her voice. He wouldn't look at her. "Stop, let me see your leg. Oh, Lord, you've got to get to the hospital. Alex!"

"I'm all right."

She tried to grab his arm. He shook her off. "What's wrong with you?" she pleaded.

He stopped, stared her in the eye. "I'm a loser."

Her mouth dropped open in amazement. "I saw how you got tripped. Those silly bitches on varsity yell were right in your way! It's a miracle you were able to finish."

"Right, a miraculous second place."

"Listen, Alex, you did the best you could. You were amazing, you really were. But now you need to get to a doctor."

"My leg is fine, Cindy," he said bitterly. "It's my head that needs a doctor."

He ignored her cries for him to come back and left

the school through a hole in the fence, walking into the woods where he could despise himself in private. Beside a tall fern, he plopped down and buried his face in his arms.

He was sitting there for approximately twenty minutes when he felt a warm hand touch his injured leg. He looked up, expecting to see his sister. Instead, he found himself staring into a wide-open pair of dark eyes.

"Joni," he muttered, surprised.

She took a new, clean white handkerchief from her pocket and began to wrap it around his cut. "Your sister wants you to have this cared for," she said.

"Did Cindy send you here?"

"No."

"Then—why are you here?"

Joni sat back on her legs. She had changed into a plain white T-shirt and red pants. Her long black hair was tied up in a ponytail. There was blood on her right hand from where she had touched him. "I enjoyed watching you run, Alex."

He lowered his gaze. "I hope you didn't enjoy watching me lose."

"I think you run better when you are chasing than when you are being chased."

He raised his head. "Huh?"

Joni smiled, her top teeth playing over her lower lip. "You should be the hunter, not the hunted."

"You mean, I shouldn't try to run in front?" He'd always done that. It was his style.

"Yes. I think you're going to win next week."

He brightened. "Maybe I will."

Joni touched his hand, squeezed it gently. Her skin was soft and warm. "Do you like me?" she asked shyly.

He blushed. "Yeah."

Joni nodded to herself, suddenly serious. "I thought so."

"Do you like me?" he asked, astounding himself.

She paused, stared at him intently for a moment. The flecks in her eyes seemed to have changed color from that morning. "Yes."

Alex began to forget about the race and the end of the world and other such nonsense. "Would you like to go to the game with me tonight?"

She pulled back slightly, glanced in the direction of the school. Alex had the impression she was considering Cindy before deciding how to answer. Her lower lip trembled slightly. "I do like you, Alex," she said.

He laughed. "Then we should go to the game together."

She hesitated. "It would be all right?"

"Sure. It would be fun."

Her smile returned. "Good."

CHAPTER

V

*I*N THE END Alex let Cindy take him to the emergency ward at Timber Memorial. He did so only under the condition she not tell their mother. His mom freaked when the least little thing happened to him. He was her baby. He never could understand why she didn't worry about Cindy in the same way.

A Dr. Harry Free put eight stitches in his knee. Cindy stayed in the room during the entire procedure —she had a strong stomach—and Alex kept his eyes glued to the ceiling. Had he not been going out with Joni that night, he probably would have gotten depressed by the whole situation. As it was, he felt fine.

The fee was one hundred and fifty dollars for twenty minutes of treatment. Their family had insurance, but they opted against using it; their parents could find out that way about his fall. Cindy had to dash over to their bank to get the dough. They were lucky it was Friday and the bank was still open. They both had solid savings accounts; their parents paid them hefty allowances for all the time they put in at the hardware store. But Cindy used her own money, insisting he didn't have to pay her back. She was real excited about his going out with Joni. When they left the hospital, they stopped at Peter's Pants, where she bought him a new shirt and pair of slacks, again using her own money. She jokingly told him that he had better get some "action" from Joni after all this trouble.

Cindy also mentioned the possibility of Joni and him accompanying Jason and herself up to Crystal Falls that evening. He wasn't enthusiastic about the idea. He didn't care for Jason, though he didn't know why exactly. Certainly, he didn't believe Jason had been responsible for Karen Holly's death. There was just something about the guy that didn't feel genuine. To dissuade Cindy, he told her about the thundershowers he had spotted way back in the mountains. She'd tell Jason about that, she said. Maybe he wouldn't want to go, after all.

The game started at six. He'd told Joni he'd pick her up at five-thirty. They didn't get back to the house until close to five. He barely had time to run into the house, stuff a roast beef sandwich in his mouth, brush his teeth, and throw on his new clothes. Cindy would be getting a ride with Pam.

"Don't treat her like she's a goddess," she warned him as he went to drive away. He assured her he'd be cool.

He was shaking when he got to the address Joni had given him. Less than two hours had gone by since he'd last seen her, and he was worrying she'd changed her mind. His leg ached as he stepped up to the front door.

You should be the hunter, not the hunted.

A kindly grandmother type answered the door.

"Mrs. Harper?" She was old to be Joni's mother.

The lady smiled. "I'm Mrs. Lee, Joni's aunt. You must be Alex. Please come in."

They went to the kitchen. He took a seat at the kitchen table. Mrs. Lee was clearing away dishes.

"We only finished dinner," she said, without a trace of her niece's accent. "Joni's still getting dressed. I'll tell her you're here in a moment."

"I'm probably early," he said, noticing Joni's schoolbooks next to him on the table.

"Joni's told me you're a runner, Alex."

"Yeah, I'm on the cross-country team."

"She also told me you're an excellent student."

"Well, I'm all right, I guess." He liked the idea of Joni talking about him. But a dark thought suddenly entered his mind. "Mrs. Lee, are you new to Timber?"

"Gracious, no, I've lived here the last twenty years with my husband. Mr. Lee's at work now, perhaps you'll meet him later. He always works late."

"Is Joni—just visiting?"

Mrs. Lee glanced over from her place at the sink. "No. Joni will be living with us from now on." She turned away, putting on the faucet. "She didn't tell you about her parents?" There was an edge in the woman's question.

"No."

Mrs. Lee stood still for a moment, then quieted the water, drying her hands with a dishtowel, returning to the table to take a seat beside him, her face pinched with concern. "It's not a matter she ever talks about. I don't know if it's something I should talk about now. But I feel I should warn you in case you were to accidentally bring it up."

"Is it something to do with her parents?"

"Yes." She paused. "They're both dead."

"That's a shame." The news did not surprise him. Since meeting Joni, he'd felt there was a shadow across her past. She possessed a "haunted" quality. It was a quality that had seemed to draw him to her. Nevertheless, he was saddened to hear the news.

Growing up without parents couldn't be easy. "When did they die?" he asked.

"Not that long ago. They— There was an accident. We were all shocked. Joni's mother was my youngest sister."

"Was Joni an only child?"

"No. She has a brother. He's—still in England." Mrs. Lee clasped her fingers together nervously. "It was a terrible accident."

"What happened?"

The woman twitched involuntarily. "It happened twice," she whispered, before suddenly twisting around to check the clock. "Oh, dear, what time does your game start?"

"Six o'clock. But that's OK, we can be late."

"I'll go see what's keeping her." Mrs. Lee stood. "I think she must have taken a shower. Wait here just a sec."

Alex decided *parents* was the last topic he would bring up that evening.

While waiting, he took a quick peek in Joni's notebook to see what she was doing in her other classes. What he found was confusing. Her Algebra I notes were a shambles. She mustn't have a mind for math, he thought, before turning to her biology papers and discovering they were in worse shape.

Mrs. Lee was back swiftly and caught him with his nose in Joni's notebook. He closed it suddenly, feeling a shade guilty. But the woman wasn't angry. She nodded sadly.

"The trauma she's been through hasn't helped her studies," she said. Then added wistfully, "And she used to do so well at school."

"I can see how losing both parents might make you lose interest in books."

"Yes, that's the problem," Mrs. Lee said hastily,

again taking a seat at the table beside him. He sensed a question that she was reluctant to ask.

"Maybe I could tutor her a couple of days a week until she gets caught back up," he offered.

Joni's aunt perked up. "Could you? You have no idea how much that would be appreciated." She lowered her voice. "Joni would never directly ask for help, you understand. Perhaps you could help her in an informal setting, here and there." She added, "We could pay you for your time."

Alex smiled. "If Joni wants tutoring, it would be my pleasure to give it to her." He was somewhat surprised at how quickly the woman had taken to him. There was a slightly desperate tone in everything she said. The grief over her sister's death must still be weighing her down.

"Alex," Joni said.

He hadn't heard her entering. She'd changed into a baggy blue skirt, and loosened her thick black hair so it twisted and curled practically to her waist. He'd never really seen her legs before. They were very shapely, and tone. She was probably a fair runner. She'd caught him easily enough.

"You look marvelous," he said, responding spontaneously, getting to his feet.

"Thank you."

Mrs. Lee hurried to Joni's side. "Did you use my dryer?" she asked, touching her niece's hair. "Can't have you catching cold."

"Yes."

"But you can't be going out like this without a coat," the aunt said. "You've seen how the mountain air changes once the sun goes down."

"I won't be cold," Joni said.

"I have a wool sweater I want you to take," Mrs. Lee said, turning for the hallway. Joni stopped her.

"I'll be fine," she said.

"I have an extra coat in the car, Mrs. Lee," Alex said.

The lady fussed nervously before forcing a big smile. "Very well, then. I do hope you kids have a good time."

Joni smiled at him. "We will," Alex said.

Cindy's legs were cold and so was her butt, even though she'd been waving the latter around all evening. Halftime was always a pain; they had to stand around the stadium in their cute little song skirts while the football team got to relax in the warm comfort of the locker room. The song team did not participate directly in the halftime show. The score was tied at fourteen. Both sides were running on every boring play and Cindy was thinking it was going to be a long season.

"I told you to quit the squad this year," Pam said as she handed Cindy a hot dog and coffee through the fence that separated the bottom row of the bleachers from the track and playing field. "Then you could be in the stands where all the action is."

Cindy sipped her coffee. "So what's happening in the stands?"

"I've got Bala with me and Alex's got Joni."

"Are you sitting with Alex?"

"A couple of rows behind them."

"How's he doing with her?"

"I saw him put an arm around her."

"For how long?"

"Just for a moment," Pam said. "It was kind of a hug."

"That's not bad, though, for a first date. Don't you think?"

"Ray was out with me only an hour and he had his hand under my bra."

"I saw Ray walk by here a moment ago."

"Don't mention that guy's name," Pam swore.

"Sorry. Where's Bala got to?"

Pam made a face, which was easy for her to do with the sort of face she had. "He wanted to go for a stroll. I don't think he's finding my company completely captivating."

"Let him go through a half dozen other girls in the school and then he'll know what he's got in you."

Pam regarded her suspiciously. "Starting with who?"

Bala walked up at that moment. Standing on the planks above Cindy, he looked about ten feet tall. The way she smiled at him, Pam could probably guess who he could start with.

"Having fun?" Cindy asked, taking a sexy bite out of her hot dog.

He filled his lungs, glancing to the right and left, at the bowl of the stadium, the bright tungsten lights and the colorful crowd, and said with a note of awe, "I have never seen anything like this in my whole life."

"Wait till we play a team that has a quarterback that can throw the ball," Pam said.

"I love those little dances you do," he told Cindy. "And those songs you sing."

"That's just lewd suggestive squirming and jock-stroking squealing," Pam said, disgusted. Cindy put on her sweet innocent expression.

"Thank you, Bala."

"Oh, Cindy, dear," Pam said in the same sugar-coated voice, turning her head toward the north end of the field. "Our young gladiators are returning to the appointed battlefield, and I do believe your personal champion is heading this way for a kiss of encouragement."

She was right. Jason, carrying his helmet, was jogging over to see her. He'd fumbled the ball twice in the first half. He might not be keen on finding her flirting with Bala for the second time in the same day. "Bala," she said. "Could you do me a favor? Could you go tell Alex I'd like to speak with him?"

Pam recognized her discomfort. "I'll go. Bala can stay here and chat with you and your *boyfriend.*"

"Bala, you go," she said. "Please?"

"Certainly," he said, leaving. She hoped he knew who Alex was.

"I think we're going to end up hating each other before Africa gets him back," Pam growled.

Jason arrived a minute later. He'd painted black chalk underneath his darling gray eyes to cut down on the glare of the lights. It made Cindy think of zebras.

"Can I have a bite of that hot dog?" he asked. Cindy gave it to him. "Brea's defensive line's got some big bastards," he remarked, stuffing the wiener in his mouth.

"I think they've been hitting you low," she said sympathetically.

"Ain't that the truth," Jason agreed, starting to give her the hot dog back. She gestured for him to finish it.

"I think they've been hitting your football too often," Pam remarked.

"Huh?" Jason said.

"That was a great run you made at the end of the first quarter," Cindy said quickly.

"I've got to make more of them in the next two quarters if we're going to win," Jason said.

Oh, no, Cindy thought. They had a new arrival.

"Hey, Jason! My man! Love the way you squirt that ball out of your hands when you're carrying it."

Ray Bower, a large Pepsi in one hand and a gallon of popcorn in the other, leaned against the rail beside his old girlfriend. Pam's eyes widened. Jason's narrowed. "If you took a single one of the hits I've been taking all night, Bower," Jason said, "you'd be in a hospital bed."

"Yeah, you're right." Ray grinned. "You're a mean hombre. You're like your namesake in *Friday the 13th.* You get up no matter how many times you're knocked down. I bet an old grizzly couldn't put you out of action."

Jason slammed his helmet onto the track. He began to climb the fence to tear Ray's head off. Cindy grabbed hold of his jersey. Pam moved in front of Ray.

"You take that back!" Jason screamed, unable to fit his cleats into the meshed wire, slipping hopelessly against the fence.

"You should be in the movies," Ray went on, taking a sip of Pepsi. "In a new series: *Jason's Younger Brother.*"

"You're dead, Bower!"

"Guys, stop it!" Cindy shouted, yanking on Jason's team number, spilling her coffee on her nylons. "Everyone's watching. Ray, you should apologize."

"I'm sorry if Jason took *personal* insult in what I just said," Ray replied, enjoying his popcorn.

"Hey, let's cool it," Pam said, obviously worried what Jason might do, now or later. Jason's face smoldered with blood.

"I'll remember that remark," Jason swore, letting go of the fence, fighting to calm himself.

"I doubt it," Ray said. "According to the papers, you've got a lousy memory."

"Stop it!" Cindy pleaded, getting upset as Jason made another lunge at the fence. She was not a crier, but she purposely let tears fill her eyes, hoping she could make the guys feel ashamed. It worked, to an extent. Jason backed off.

"There'll be another time, Bower," he muttered, picking up his helmet.

"There's a week from Monday at your preliminary hearing," Ray said ominously.

Bala returned with Alex and Joni. That sure had been quick; her brother must have been sitting in the lower bleachers. She'd sent Bala away because she didn't want him around when she was with Jason. Now she felt the reverse; if hostilities erupted again, his strong black arms would be able to restore order. Alex noticed her eyes were red.

"What's wrong?" he asked.

"Jason's been playing basketball with his helmet," Ray said. "Almost brought tears to my own eyes."

Alex scowled at Ray. "You been starting a fight again?"

"Actually, I have, yes."

"Let's ignore him and maybe he'll undergo spontaneous human combustion," Pam said.

"Good idea," Jason said, turning to her. "Is tonight still on?"

"Alex said he saw a thunderstorm brewing back in the mountains," Cindy said.

"Were the clouds over Castle Park?" Jason asked Alex. A couple of teammates on the bench called for Jason to come over. He waved them away.

"No, they were way back. But the park will be getting the run off."

Jason smiled. "That's good. The falls will be full of water. You should come with us, Alex. Show your girl Wyoming's most scenic spot."

"Where is this?" Joni asked. Cindy noted with

pleasure how close Joni stood to Alex, making it clear to everyone she was with him. And she was wearing his jacket.

"There's a national park about half an hour drive from here," Alex explained. "There's a waterfall there you can hike up to. Does that sound like fun?"

Joni nodded. "I like the outdoors."

"We would be out late if we go," Alex warned.

"It doesn't matter," Joni said.

"I have never seen a waterfall," Bala said.

"But they showed lots of them in the movie *Out of Africa,*" Pam said in disbelief.

"I have never seen a movie," Bala said innocently. "Could we, too, go to this place?"

"Sure," Jason said. "We'll all go."

"I hope you won't mind me riding with you, Jason," Ray said.

"Ray," Pam told him, "if Jason took you, you'd probably end up walking home."

"With two broken legs," Jason agreed.

Ray lost his carefree snicker. "I couldn't complain about that," he said seriously. "Not after what happened to Karen." He turned, preparing to leave, when he seemed to notice for the first time that Joni was with Alex. He went to speak again, thought better of it, and then simply walked away.

"Who's Karen?" Bala asked.

"Just a girl." Cindy sighed, feeling a chill.

CHAPTER
VI

JASON FUMBLED ONCE MORE in the third quarter, but all was forgiven when he broke through in the last two minutes of the fourth quarter for a five-yard touchdown to put Timber High up to stay: 21 to 20. He was in a much better mood after the game than he had been at halftime.

The three pairs ended up going in separate cars to Castle Park; that way, on the trip home, they wouldn't have to return to the school. Since her legs were yelling for a pair of warm pants, Cindy had Jason swing by her house. The others would just have to wait. They had arranged to meet at Lot H.

Inside, her parents were enjoying the latest episode of "Dallas." Her dad got all excited when he heard about Jason's run at the end of the game. He promised he would be at the game next Friday. Cindy was not overjoyed at the prospect. She always felt inhibited cheering when her father was watching.

Cindy did not tell her folks about Alex's fall and subsequent visit to the hospital, but did mention his hot date. Her mother was delighted and started pumping her for information about Joni. Cindy warned them Alex might be bringing Joni back to the house for a snack, and that they should remain in bed like good little parents. She didn't say exactly where they were all going that night.

Wolf needed walking and Cindy wanted his protection, so the big dog joined their party. Jason began to wonder about her paranoia when they were walking to his Camaro—his Jaguar was in the shop—and she suddenly jogged into the garage and returned with a rifle and a box of cartridges. The caliber of the gun was high enough to stop an elephant.

"If you tried firing that thing," he said as they pulled away, "you'd probably take your shoulder off."

"I'm an expert shot," she said honestly. "I could hit a Coke can at a hundred yards with this rifle."

He knew she wasn't one to brag, and was impressed. "Where did you learn to do that?"

Wolf perched over from the backseat and licked the side of her face. She patted him on the top of the head and pointed out the window. A week-old moon hung above the treetops, its light shining like a peaceful celestial tonic over the whole valley. "See that target up there?"

"What? The moon?"

"When I was in about fourth grade, my dad would take me outside at night with a rifle and a pair of binoculars and have me shoot at the moon. After each shot, I would check in the binoculars to see if there were any new craters. That would mean I had hit it. I must have known I wasn't really shooting the moon, but it seemed after each shot, I'd see an extra crater."

"Why did he have you do that?"

"I think it was his way of telling me at that impressionable age that the moon was the only safe thing to shoot at. Of course, later we practiced on cans and bottles. My dad has always been big on me being able to protect myself. He helped me train Wolf."

"I'm glad you told me all this." Jason smiled. "I'll be sure to move carefully around you."

She touched his leg. "I don't want you being too careful," she said slyly.

He shook his head. "You amaze me, Cindy. I don't know how you've put up with me lately. I've been so disgusted with all the talk that's been going on at school, I've been perpetually pissed off. Tonight was a perfect example. If you, and the fence, hadn't been there, I don't know what I would have done to Ray."

A feeling of warmth for him flowed through her. Caught in the light of the moon, she thought his profile adorable. He was much more relaxed, going to this place where all his troubles had started, than he had been since school had begun. It was easy to remember all the reasons she liked him: his great eyes, his confidence, his sharp mind, his great mouth. She leaned over and kissed him on the cheek. "Let's not worry about any of that stuff tonight," she said.

The toughness of the soles of Joni's feet amazed Alex. They were almost to the top of Pathfinders Trail—with Cindy and Jason ahead, and Pam and Bala bringing up the rear—and she had yet to complain about a sharp pebble or jagged pine needle. He was still mad at himself for his lack of foresight. But it had only been when they had reached Lot H, and were waiting around for the others to show, that he had realized Joni couldn't possibly hike to the top of the waterfall in high heels. No problem, she had said, taking off her shoes. Apparently, she liked to go barefoot.

The night was beautiful and Alex was happy. Off to their left, falling a steep and rocky two thousand feet, was the gorge the swift and patient Snake Tail River had cut over the last couple of ice ages. And the waterfall was not far ahead, its cold water sparkling in the moonlight, the roar of its crashing foam filling their ears.

"We're almost there," he told Joni. Their path was partially protected from the harsh surroundings, with intertwined tree branches creating a natural ceiling above their heads. Joni was holding his hand and her fingers were delightfully warm. "Are you getting tired?"

"No," she said.

He was. The race that afternoon and the stitches in his knee had slowed him a spell. But it was a pleasant fatigue. He was thinking of the look Ray had given him when he had realized Joni was with him. It was rare to see Ray shocked.

"Did you enjoy the game?" he asked. She hadn't appeared to understand the rules.

"The boys looked like they were trying to hurt each other."

He laughed, quickly changing his mind. She had understood in one night what most people in the audience never did after years of watching, he thought.

Cindy was slowing and they caught up with her and Jason a few minutes later. Wolf was giving Cindy an awful time; the dog was unusually nervous and kept darting off the path.

"I should never have brought him," she grumbled, searching the foliage. "Wolf! Wolf!"

The dog did not appear, and they waited for better than two minutes. Cindy started to worry. "Jason, could something have happened to him?" she asked.

"If he slipped and broke a leg, you'd hear him howling," Jason said.

"There he is." Alex pointed. Wolf was trudging

happily beside Bala, who, along with Pam, was finally catching up with them. Alex was surprised; the dog didn't normally take to strangers.

"If you don't start behaving," Cindy said, scolding the dog, "you're eating dog food for the next two weeks. Now keep beside me."

Wolf was not impressed. As they continued their hike, the dog continued to stay near Bala.

They reached the top of the falls not long after, and took a breather on a boulder next to where the river went over the edge. The view was glorious. Had Jason not been keen to press on, Alex thought, they would've been content to stay where they were.

Looking straight down over the falls was enough to get one's head spinning. The mighty shower fell nearly two hundred feet into a churning rock-rimmed bowl that gave the impression of having a giant creature deep within its bowels, fighting to enter the world of the living.

"How deep is that lake down there?" Bala asked.

"That isn't a lake," Pam said, unusually quiet, probably because she was tired from the hike. "It's a whirlpool."

"It's deep enough that one guy thought he could go over the falls in a barrel and live," Jason said.

"When was that?" Cindy asked.

"Five years ago," Jason said.

"Did he drown?" Bala asked.

"He broke his neck," Jason said and then he did a very unexpected thing. He had carried Cindy's father's rifle from the car, and now, suddenly, he raised it to his shoulder, reaching for the trigger. "This gorge has incredible acoustics. Listen to this. I'm going to shoot Cindy's moon."

"Jason, no!" Cindy screamed.

Her warning came too late. The gun was fired, and

before the boom could even begin to reverberate through the rocky valley, Wolf attacked Jason.

Seeing the dog come, Jason immediately threw up his arm. Wolf went for that instead of the throat. Since the dog couldn't finish Jason by ripping out his arteries, it decided to finish him by shoving him over the side of the cliff.

"Heel! Heel!" Cindy shouted, moving quickly to grab Wolf by the neck. The dog had gone wild. Guns always had that effect on him. He ignored Cindy's command, and Jason staggered backward, moving closer and closer to the edge, a row of teeth clamped around his right elbow.

Then the crisis ended almost before it began.

A small miracle happened. A high-pitched shrill whistle sounded above the roar of the falls. And Wolf let go of Jason.

Come again? Alex thought.

Wolf turned and ran to Bala, who grabbed the dog by the thick fur at the back of the neck. It had been Bala who had made the strange whistle. Wolf licked his face to show he could whistle more if he wanted.

Cindy snatched her boyfriend back to safety. "Are you OK?" she asked anxiously, hugging Jason. "I should've warned you sooner. Oh, God, you could have gone over the side! How's your arm? Are you bleeding? That damn dog."

Jason was shook, but no one was going to say he didn't have good reason. "I'm fine," he said, feeling his arm while keeping an eye on Wolf. "Your dog's got violent reflexes."

"Those sure are incredible acoustics, Jason," Pam said with a nervous laugh. Standing to her left, Joni appeared unmoved by the incident.

"Hey, Bala," Alex said. "What was that you whistled?"

"Yeah, how did you do that?" Cindy asked, quickly regaining control of herself. She let go of Jason and stepped toward Bala. He knelt and fluffed Wolf's hairy head.

"It was nothing," he said.

"It was definitely something," Cindy said. "I've raised this dog since he was a puppy. Why did he react so quickly to your whistle?"

Bala smiled. "I have always had a way with animals."

"Did your grandfather teach you this *way?*" Cindy asked.

Bala lowered his head. "Yes, he did. When I was young."

Cindy leaned over and gave Bala a brief hug. "Well, thank your grandfather for me. He just might have saved Jason's life."

The hug appeared to embarrass Bala. "I will, when I see him," he said.

"Yeah, thanks Bala," Jason said with an eye on Cindy. "You've got to teach me that whistle someday."

"It is not something you can learn in a day," Bala said.

Pam turned away, shaking her head. "Since when does Wolf understand bush language?" she muttered.

Cindy would have preferred to call it a night. She was tired and it wasn't getting any earlier. But Jason was adamant about going on. There was a cave he wanted her to see.

She couldn't remember any cave in the area.

The gang had been reshuffled. The guys were walking on ahead, as guys are prone to do when their female companions start to get tired. Wolf was sticking with Bala. Cindy had been surprised Alex had parted from Joni's side. Perhaps he felt a responsibility to scout on ahead and make sure all was safe. No one knew this place like Alex. He was carrying the gun now.

Rain clouds continued to linger over the distant mountains, from which could be heard an occasional rumble of thunder. The river was two hundred yards off to their left, fat with the storm's fresh downpour. Few trees could be found at this elevation, and the light of the moon shown unobstructed. A roughly chiseled granite mound protruded on their immediate left. Cindy remembered Kent Cooke's article.

"Do you know where we are?" Cindy asked Pam.

"I'm not sure," Pam said uneasily.

"This is the spot," Joni said, her voice a bit heavy, as though she were just getting over a cold.

Cindy looked at her. "Are you sure?"

Joni nodded. "Karen died right here."

Cindy wasn't inclined to question her sources. "Ray didn't sound like himself when he mentioned Karen tonight," she said to Pam.

"I suppose he had his reasons," Pam said, obviously not wanting to discuss this in front of Joni. She'd made her point, anyway. It had been a strange match, but Ray and Karen had actually dated for several months. This had been before Ray and Pam had become an item. This was probably another reason Ray and Jason were not bosom buddies. Joni must have sensed the undercurrent of the discussion.

"Karen was a wonderful friend to me," she said suddenly.

Cindy felt slightly ashamed. She had known Karen —known *of* her, at least—for years and couldn't say the same. "It must have been a terrible shock for you, to just meet her and all, and then to have her taken away?"

Joni regarded her thoughtfully, the large moon reflecting with uncanny clarity in her big black eyes. "I often dream of Karen in this place." She lowered her thick lashes. "It makes me sad."

They were heading due north, cutting directly in between a loop in the river. Consequently, it wasn't too long before they were again beside the water. The guys had stopped and were waiting.

"Almost there," Jason said, holding their unused flashlight.

"Where exactly is this cave?" Alex asked, scrutinizing the narrow bank of the river as it wrapped precariously between the water and the stone walls, the latter rising higher and higher the farther you went back into the mountains.

Jason nodded. "Around this bend. I'll show you." He stretched out his hand to Cindy. She still felt self-conscious holding Jason's hand in front of Bala. The demonstration of Bala's ability to handle Wolf—and she had a sneaking suspicion he could handle *any* animal—made her even more reluctant. His aura of mystery had deepened in her eyes; she knew this was making him more enticing to her.

She shoved the thought away and took Jason's hand.

"The bank is smooth and narrow here," Alex said. "It may even be wet. I don't know if this cave is worth it."

Jason was thinking. The rest of them were waiting for another opinion. Bala spoke next. "I'll go first. I'm quick on my feet. I'll be able to see how safe it is."

"No," Jason said firmly. "I'll lead the way. I'm familiar with the terrain." He chuckled. "We're beginning to sound like we're going off to war. Come on, Cindy." He tugged on her hand and then dropped it.

She was wearing a pair of leather high-top basketball shoes. She'd found them preferable to ordinary hiking boots; they supported her ankles over rough ground while still being flexible enough not to throw off her natural stride. The soles of the shoes had an excellent grip. Following Jason along the narrow stone path that ran about ten feet above the rushing water, with Bala at her back, Cindy felt secure. If her balance were to waver, there were ample branches sticking out from the wall on her right to grab. But she was concerned about Joni in her bare feet.

Cindy was turning to check on Joni when she slipped.

Instinctively, Cindy's right hand shot out and grabbed a thick branch. It must have been dead and dried. It snapped, and she was falling. For the tiniest instant, just before the icy water engulfed her, Cindy thought she felt Bala's fingers touching her wrist.

Oh, God, no!

The cold was black and strong. She was going down and being swept backward. The fall had caught her without a solid breath. Her lungs screamed for air. She flailed blindly with her arms, her flesh cringing in the grip of the current. Her leg slapped a rock, then another. She kicked upward. Her head broke the surface.

"Alex!" Cindy screamed.

They were receding from her at a frightening speed, but even with her hair plastered over her face, she could see them clearly. Her terror sharpened her eyesight, so that the moonlight appeared far more brilliant. The group got jammed on the narrow bank as they all tried to chase after her. Alex was the first to emerge from the tangle.

"Swim toward the side!" he yelled, running downstream at approximately the same speed she was being swept away. Almost as soon as she had entered the water, she had been sucked to the center of the river. She tried to do as he suggested. Her soaked sweatshirt made her feel as though she were swimming in molasses. The bank was getting no closer. A crosscurrent was resisting her.

"Alex!" she cried, water splashing down her throat, making her gag.

"I'll catch you downstream, Cindy!" Jason yelled, drawing up beside Alex. She thought she understood what he meant and had her guess confirmed when she saw him beginning to cut inland, away from the water. The river looped. He was going to run across the ground they had just covered, going downstream way ahead of her, and wait for her to come to him. She didn't like that plan. If he were to miss her there, only a few seconds would be left before she'd go over the falls.

"No!" She coughed, continuing to flail with her arms, her strength draining. The intense cold was to blame. There was snow back in the mountains that hadn't melted all summer. The rain water must have run over it. Her muscles were literally freezing up.

"I'll save you!" Jason promised, breaking away from Alex and Bala—who had joined in the pursuit. He disappeared into the night. Alex and Bala were running side by side. They were no longer shouting to her but were talking between themselves. First Alex shook his head, then Bala shook his. It was an awful time, Cindy thought, for them to be unable to come to an agreement. More submerged stones struck her feet and legs, one so hard she felt it must have shattered her ankle. But the pain up her leg did not last long. Her feet were going numb.

"Help!" she wailed.

The river was picking up speed, narrowing. Up ahead, she could hear the roar of Crystal Falls.

"Alex!"

Alex and Bala both vanished. A cluster of trees and boulders had forced them away from the edge of the water. Cindy began to panic. A shrewdly calculating part of her brain was telling her that the odds were that she would be going flying very soon.

Karen went this same way.

But Karen had been dead before she had been thrown in the water. Cindy strove harder with her leaden arms. She was not going to give up.

A couple of minutes went by—and *a lot* of ground. Alex finally reappeared. He was alone. He was pulling off his coat, preparing to dive into the water.

"Stay! Stay!" she yelled. All the time she had been screaming for her brother to save her, she had meant that Jason and Bala should do it. "Don't, Alex!"

He wasn't listening, striding swiftly into the water, being picked up off his feet and sucked into the current. He was much closer to the bank than she was, and at least a hundred feet farther upstream, but suddenly she had hope. Alex was an excellent swimmer. He plowed toward her.

"Hang on!" he said.

The force of the current appeared to be split down the middle of the river. Alex drew even with her but was unable to make it across a vicious invisible eddy.

"Cindy! Try swimming toward the other side!"

She understood the logic of his advice. Yet it was next to impossible to convince her exhausted limbs to head away from her only source of help. The approaching falls sounded like thunder in her ears.

"Get back to the side!" she shouted.

"Turn! Go the other way!" Alex shouted back. "Use your legs as well as your arms!"

She decided her only choice was to do what he said. But as she turned, a tall dark figure caught her eye.

Bala was standing on a cliff above where Alex and she would soon pass. He was removing his shirt. How he had gotten all the way up there in so short a time was beyond Cindy.

As she watched, he retreated from the edge of the cliff, vanishing. For an instant her heart stopped beating. A second miracle from him in the same night would have been too much to ask. She asked, anyway.

God, please!

Suddenly he reappeared, running at an incredible speed, leaping off the cliff. He seemed to hang in the air forever, falling in slow motion. He hit the water not ten yards from her. But he did not resurface, and she waited, and waited—

A strong arm wrapped around her side and a large black head popped up a few inches from her gasping mouth.

"My grandfather also taught me how to swim," Bala said.

"And how to fly?" she choked.

"Alex, I have her," Bala called. "Return to your side."

Alex waved, turning away from them. Bala tightened his grip on her, actually lifting her several inches above the water. He must have had incredibly powerful legs. He began to take long even strokes with his free arm.

"Hurry," she whispered. The point where the river transformed into Crystal Falls had become visible. Between them and it lay a huge fallen tree. To her further amazement and horror she saw Jason was hanging from the tree *by his knees,* waiting to swoop them to safety. Bala saw him, too.

"Jason, get off there!" he yelled.

Jason checked in the direction of the falls, then appeared to mentally measure the distance between them and the opposite side of the river. "You won't make it!" he yelled back. "Swim more toward the center!"

Cindy wouldn't have known which option to take: hope Jason would catch them as they whisked by or hope they could make it to the shore. Bala had no doubt about the matter; he was going for the opposite shore. He ignored several pleas of Jason's to reverse directions. A few seconds later, they floated beneath the tree, far beyond Jason's hanging reach.

"You're crazy, Bala!" he swore. "Cindy!"

Bala didn't reply. He was saving his breath, moving them toward the side, foot by blessed foot. The water of the river had quickened, anticipating the big plunge that was coming. For Cindy, it was like drowning at the edge of the world. She squeezed her eyes tightly shut, wishing she could wake up in her bed at home.

I cannot die. I will not die.

An eternity of slow seconds went by. Then a wave slammed against her, and kept slamming.

"Cindy, open your eyes," Bala said.

She did as she was told. He had reached the side, and was hanging on to a narrow crack in the stone wall. The wave was from the force of the river; while moving with it, she hadn't truly felt its pressure.

"I am going to have to let you go," Bala said.

Cindy glanced over her shoulder. The floor of the gorge was waiting with wide-open arms. "I think that would be a very bad idea," she said.

Bala was firm. "I have to let you go to climb up this rock. See, there are many places you can hold. When I reach the top, I will be able to pull you up."

She nodded. "OK." He was right; there were many places to grab hold.

"Keep a good hold, Cindy," he cautioned, reaching to pull himself up.

"You be careful, yourself," she said between chattering teeth.

Bala could not only talk to dogs and swim like a fish, he could climb walls like a fly. He was up and over the top in the blink of an eye. His head poked over a moment later.

"Cindy, you're going to have to move down about thirty feet."

"Why?"

"I need a place to wrap my feet around in order to pull you up."

"Do you mean I have to move in the direction of the waterfall?" The edge was only fifty feet away.

"Yes."

"Maybe I should just try to climb up. You did it easily enough."

"You are not me."

She couldn't argue with that. The rock appeared equipped with ample handles. Carefully, more carefully than she had ever done anything in her life, she crept toward the brink.

We should have just gone for pizza.

The river made one last stab at her life. She was in position and reaching up, with Bala leaning over the side with practically the entire length of his body, when a log—it was really lousy timing on the log's part—hit her flush on the shoulder. The jolt made her anchoring fingers slip.

"Bala!" she cried.

His hand closed on her wrist like a vise. Seemingly without effort, he pulled her up to the point where she could make it the rest of the way on her own. When she was safe, she saw that his toes were dug around a sharp ripple in the stone. His entire weight was being supported by the equivalent of a thread. Yet he waved her away when she started to grab his legs. He could manage very well on his own, thank you. You'd think she would know that by now.

"Does your grandfather like to go for late-night swims?" she asked when he was upright once more. She was trembling violently, her breath coming in ragged gulps.

Bala laughed, loud and deep. "Not as much as you do, Cindy."

I'm alive.

The truth of the simple thought filled her with wonder. She collapsed against him, pressing into the warmth of his body. Hesitantly, he wrapped his arm around her. He had stripped off his shirt for her rescue. He was as wet as herself. But he was not shivering, nor did he even seem to notice the cold.

"I owe you my life," she said.

He shook his head, glancing at the moon. "Do not feel in my debt. One day, you never know, you might feel you have to pay me back. And that would not be good."

Alex did not go careening by and Cindy therefore knew he must have made it to safety. Jason appeared shortly after, on the other side of the top of the falls, and confirmed that her brother was indeed fine. Jason did this by arm gestures. Talk across the deafening noise of the water was impossible.

An exhilarating euphoria began to fill Cindy. She'd read about such experiences from people who had just missed meeting the Grim Reaper. A shame you had to go to such extremes to get the happiness hormone flowing. She wouldn't mind feeling this way all the time—as if she could fly.

Alex and Joni arrived beside Jason a few minutes later. Joni had removed the coat Alex had lent her earlier and wrapped it around his shoulders. Alex appeared to be sharing her joy at their near escape from the clutches of death; he kept bouncing up and down. Or maybe he was just trying to stay warm.

Pam was the last to put in an appearance. She'd thoughtfully collected Alex and Bala's coats, plus the rifle Alex had dropped when the mad chase had started. Her excited waves were easy for Cindy to decipher. Pam was glad she was alive, too.

Not far from where they had parked was the sole bridge over the river. It was obvious to both sides they would have to split up until they reached it. Cindy thought the others might be waiting for a while. The blow her ankle had taken from the underwater boulder appeared serious. As their two groups went their respective ways, she was limping badly. Bala immediately offered to carry her.

"It's four miles back down," she said. "You couldn't possibly carry me all that way."

He crouched over and swooped her off the ground. "I have carried heavier women," he said.

"Whoa! You mean, I'm not your first?" she teased, leaning her head against the smooth hardness of his chest.

"I used to carry my mother to her bath. That was three miles in the heat. Even when she was sick, she weighed more than you do now."

"She was sick? What was wrong with her?"

"Cholera. We had an epidemic of it. Killed many of my people." He added, "But my mother was spared."

"She's still alive today?"

"Yes."

"Do you miss her?"

"When I think about her, I feel close to her; I know she is thinking of me, too."

"How about your father?"

"He died. But not from cholera. It happened when I was much younger. When I was a boy."

His voice wavered when he spoke of his father. She decided to change the subject. "I loved that story you told in class today," she said.

"I did not tell much."

The noise of the waterfall was receding. The air was still, without a trace of a breeze. "Yes, you did. And you told me more tonight. I've watched you. You have magic. That boy who went into those animals, that was you, wasn't it?"

Bala didn't answer immediately and she worried that she had tread where she was not welcome. "Why do you say this?" he asked finally.

"Bala, I didn't mean to pry. I—"

"No, your question is not offensive. But why do you I say I was this boy?"

"You speak English as well, if not better, than I do."

He smiled. "And which animal taught me this?"

"I mean, you have an extraordinary mind." *Not to mention an extraordinary body.* "Why do you sometimes sound ashamed of being a Bairavee?"

The moon had slipped behind a cloud and the landscape had darkened. Bala's stride was long and tireless. Cindy wasn't worried he would stumble.

"You said I have magic, Cindy. I have read your definition of that word. I do not believe in it. No one is magically given what he wants in life. Even my grandfather has to earn what comes to him. Or pay for it."

"What do you mean?"

Bala took a deep breath. "My father died trying to learn my grandfather's craft."

"I'm sorry," she muttered, not knowing what else to say.

Bala shifted her in his arms. "You love to hear of Bairavees, Cindy. That is unusual in this country. I think *you* have the extraordinary mind. I will sing you a Bairavee song. Listen closely; you can learn more that way than by asking questions."

"Bala?"

"Shh. Listen."

He began to sing. His voice, though soft and deep, was very powerful. She imagined it carrying far, over and around the trees and rocks, into the sky. In some way it seemed to her his song was *coming* from the outside, and that he was merely reciting it back to an earth that already knew its meaning.

She hugged closer to his body. He had magic, the fool, he just didn't know it. His skin was as warm as if a bright sun were beating down upon it. And the warmth was seeping into her, into her blood. The stinging in her ankle receded, as did the rest of the world. She could hear his song, that was enough. Listening and floating, she knew she could learn a lot.

She didn't remember when she fell asleep.

CHAPTER
VII

I DON'T KNOW if my nervous system could take many more days like this, Alex thought as he pulled into his driveway, still dripping wet, Joni still by his side. He had run his legs off, crash-landed on the asphalt, been humiliated by his friend, gone out with the girl of his dreams, and fought to save his sister from death. He was surprised when he checked his watch; it was only one in the morning.

"Are you sure you're not tired?" he asked Joni before turning off the ignition. "I could take you straight home?"

"I feel fine."

Alex had to agree she looked fine; the long walks and the evening's drama had not ruffled her feathers in the slightest. "Your aunt won't be worried about you?"

"My aunt worries about me when I'm home in bed."

Alex turned off the engine and opened the door, letting Wolf out, who, to his surprise, promptly ran into the trees and disappeared. Probably had to attend to a call of nature, he decided, not giving the matter a second thought. He was anxious to get out of his soggy clothes. "Let's go in, then. I don't think my parents will still be up."

He was glad his guess proved accurate. His mom would've wanted to know why he was all wet. His dad would've been winking at him after taking one good look at Joni. The first thing Alex did was close the door to the hallway leading to their bedroom.

"Do you like tea?" he asked, turning to look at Joni as she stood silently in the kitchen. The lower hem of her dress was damp. When he had pulled himself gasping from the river, she'd been there to help him. That had been a terrible moment; he hadn't known if Bala would be able to rescue Cindy. He shuddered at the memory.

"Very much."

He stepped past her, feeling her eyes on him. "I'll put on the kettle. The water should be boiling by the time I get back. I'm just going to make a quick change."

Upstairs in his bedroom, with his pants off, he discovered he had reopened half the stitches in his knee. He decided that was a small price to have paid for Cindy's safety, though of course he realized he hadn't done a damn thing to help. Bala and his incredible athletic ability were to thank. Bala might not know it yet, but he had a friend for life in Alex Jones.

Bala versus Jason? My sister's blind.

Alex hadn't been too pleased with Jason's behavior once the crisis was over. Walking back down the mountain, with Cindy and Bala on the other side, Jason had rambled on about what a fool Bala had been not to let him pluck Cindy up to safety from the overhanging tree. Alex had finally had to tell him to shut up. Then, when they had joined up with Bala, and discovered Cindy asleep in his arms, Jason had reacted with typical immature jealousy. He'd insisted Cindy be awakened, that she could walk the rest of the way. He'd only backed down when Bala had explained how painful her ankle was, and how much the experience had worn her out. It had sure burned Jason up watching Bala carry Cindy all the way to the car, knowing he didn't have the strength to do it. Then, finally, at the parking lot, Jason had ignored Bala and Alex's recommendation that Cindy be taken straight home.

Jason's probably trying to convince Cindy right now that it was Bala's idea to go to the cave.

Cindy sure had been zonked. She hadn't even awakened when Jason had strapped the seat belt across her chest. It was as though she had been sedated.

Alex got a roll of sterile gauze from the bathroom next to his bedroom—his knee was bleeding slightly and beginning to sting a lot—and began to worry whether he should try to kiss Joni. He wanted to; he had sure thought about it enough since school had begun. But he didn't know how to get started. He sort of doubted the opportunity would simply present itself. He didn't even know if he would recognize the opportunity should he be so fortunate. He wondered if he should brush his teeth again.

Joni was pouring the boiling water into the teapot when he returned to the kitchen. Watching her complete the simple task, he realized again why he found her so attractive. Her beauty was only a part of it; she had grace. She only had to walk across the room and anyone could tell she came from a different universe from the other girls at school.

He smiled. "How did you find the tea?"

"The container gives off an aroma." She glanced past him. "You haven't introduced me to your girlfriend."

Alex turned. "You mean Sybil? She usually introduces herself." He stepped over to his old yellow parrot, Joni coming up at his side, her long hair brushing against his arm. "Sybil, say hello to Joni."

"Hello, Sybil," the bird chirped.

"Sometimes she can learn a new name in a single session. Except my sister's. For some reason, she refuses to say Cindy's name." Alex bent again to the cage. "Joni—Joni—She's really old, really smart." He didn't see any point in saying she was also blind; it might make Joni sad. "Say Joni, Sybil. Joni—Joni—"

"Hello, Alex," the bird replied.

Joni smiled, a larger smile than he had ever seen on her face. "Can I talk to her?"

"Certainly, just don't put your fingers—"

Through the wire. Damn it!

Like Cindy's warning earlier about her pet, his was too late. Joni had poked her hand inside the cage and Sybil had immediately pecked at it. A dark red drop spilled over the long nail of Joni's index finger.

"Joni, are you OK?" he asked, feeling like the entire evening had probably just been ruined. "I was going to warn you to keep your distance, though she seldom bites anybody." He scolded Sybil. "You are a stupid bird!"

"Hello, Joni," Sybil said.

"Don't get upset, Alex. It's her nature."

Alex went to fetch a bandage—they seemed to be needing a lot of them lately—but Joni didn't use it, preferring to hold the cut until it stopped bleeding, which it did a moment later. Leaving the kitchen with their cups of tea, Joni patted the top of Sybil's cage.

"Joni," the bird said again.

They ended up on the couch. Joni sat down after him and she sat very close. She would've had to have sat on his lap to get any closer. Her skirt was riding up over half of her thigh. Alex sipped his tea and wished it was whiskey. And he didn't even drink.

"Quite a night we had," he remarked for something to say.

Joni nodded, trying her tea. "I had fun."

"So did I." He chuckled. "Except when my sister went in the water. Boy, I have to admit, I was scared. If anything had happened to her, I don't know if I could have taken it."

Joni took another drink of her tea and then placed the cup on a saucer on the coffee table. "I wasn't worried. I knew Bala would save her."

The remark surprised him. He'd received the impression she wasn't crazy about Bala. "How could you be so sure?"

She casually brushed at something in his hair. "Because he is so sure of himself."

"What do you mean?"

Joni's fingers lingered near his ear. "Let's not talk about him."

"OK." Her touching him tickled. "What would you like to talk about? Ah, do you have any hobbies?"

"Yes. My hobby now is doing all the things every other girl my age does."

She must be referring to the period of mourning she had just gone through, he thought, and of her desire to start again on a normal life. "I hope I can help you practice that hobby," he said, feeling pleased at the gall of the remark. Joni nodded seriously.

"I hope so, too." She slipped her hand onto the back of his neck.

"How are you doing in your classes?" he asked quickly.

"Not good." She placed her other hand on his knee. "I could help you, maybe, if you want?"

"That would be nice." She paused. "Alex, let me see your eyes."

He looked directly at her, something he had hesitated to do while sitting so close. There was a lamp on over her left shoulder, the only light on in the room. It cast a shadow across most of her face. She moistened her lips with the tip of her tongue.

"You have a lot of feeling in your eyes," she said.

He chuckled again. "Me? My eyes are very plain. It's yours that are exotic. I bet if you tried, you could become a successful model."

Joni shook her head, still serious. "My eyes are flat. They have no personality. They have only what—" She stopped herself, suddenly grinned. "I was going to say something, but I think I'll say something else."

"What?"

She moved so close he could feel her breath. "Kiss me."

"What?"

"I want you to kiss me."

Alex decided he wouldn't get a better hint all night. He kissed her and it was *something*. He had heard that nothing could compete with your imagination, but a priest had probably said it. The real Joni had a mile and then some on his fantasy Joni. Their arms went around each other. Her mouth pressed against his and she pulled him toward her and they slowly sank into the couch. Her lips were incredibly warm; it was almost as though she were hot with a fever. They stretched out on the couch. A part of him could not believe what was happening. Minutes of delight went by. The smell and taste of her filled his senses. He ran his fingers through her hair, down her back. She sighed softly, finally drawing her head slightly back.

"You're nice," she whispered. "Too nice."

92

He smiled, his courage growing in quantum leaps. "I might not be everything I appear."

She thought about that, gave him a quick peck, then leaned back again. "This is dangerous."

Was she referring to the possibility of them going all the way? Yes, that could be dangerous. He could have a heart attack. "This whole night has had its dangers," he said.

"Your sister loves you very much."

He caressed her cheek. "Why do you say that now?"

"Because I—I thought of it," she said, burying her face in his chest so that the top of her head pressed against his chin. "Alex, do you ever get hungry for something you can't have? Something you're not supposed to have?"

At the moment, he was in touch with that kind of hunger. "Yes."

"What do you do when that happens?"

"Usually? Usually I don't do anything."

"Then what happens?"

"Nothing. And my life always goes on. I suppose it always will."

She tilted her face up, touched near his right eye. "When I do nothing, I feel like—"

"Alex, is that you?"

Splendid! Splendid! Damn it!

It was his mother. He rocketed into a sitting position, almost tossing Joni onto the floor in the process. With relief, he saw his mother hadn't actually entered the living room. She was standing on the other side of the partially open hallway door, the door he had closed all the way when he had entered the house.

"Yeah," he croaked.

"Is Cindy back yet?"

"She should be in soon."

"OK, dear, just checking. Have a good night. Sweet dreams."

"Good night, Mom." Cindy must have told her he might be bringing a girl back to the house. That was the only explanation he could think of for his mom not bursting in on them. He would have to thank Cindy in the morning.

The spell had been broken. He could sense it without having to ask. Joni was sitting quietly on the couch, fixing her skirt. Her face had regained its normal distant expression.

"What were you going to say, Joni?"

She smiled faintly, sort of sadly. "Nothing."

It was a pity; she had really begun to open up. Well, there would always be another time. On the whole, the evening had exceeded his greatest expectations. "Would you like me to give you a ride home?"

Joni nodded.

She felt hot and sticky. Warm air was circulating over her legs, but at the same time she seemed to be sitting in a puddle. The awakening was a strange one. Not only did she at first have no idea where she was, she had no idea *who* she was. Opening her eyes, she glanced about, feeling a stiffness in her neck. The world came into focus slowly. She was in a car. The heater was on. The car had just stopped in a driveway. It belonged to Jason Whitfield. He was her boyfriend. *Yeah, this is the right planet.*

"Are you awake, Cindy?" Jason asked.

"Yeah, I'm here," she mumbled, sitting up, her back cracking. "How long have I been asleep?"

"Bala said you blacked out a few minutes after leaving the waterfall. Don't you remember?"

"I remember him singing—" And she remembered

almost dying. "Did he carry me all the way back to the car?"

"We both did. You didn't even stir. What did he do, hit you over the head with a club?"

"Huh?"

"Nothing." Jason opened his car door. "Let's get inside."

Jason's house was the biggest in Timber. The architecture was simple and beautiful; two stories set in a rectangle around a large central pool. Old red bricks made up the exterior walls, with ivy clinging from the flower beds to the eaves, giving the residence a traditional eastern flavor. Jason's rooms—yes, he had more than one—were on the south corner. Her ankle throbbed as she limped up the driveway.

"Can I help you?" he asked, offering his hand.

"No, I can manage."

"You might want to have that X-rayed."

"I'll be all right. Why are we here? What time is it?"

Jason opened the door to his well-lit game room. He smiled. "I thought you could use some hot chocolate after your cold bath."

"That sounds good." She nodded, staggering inside, searching around for a frumpy chair she wouldn't mind getting all wet. Naturally, she didn't find any; there was no second-hand furniture in the Whitfield residence.

"Why don't you get out of those clothes?" Jason asked, watching her.

"I've nothing to change into."

Jason smiled again. "Wear one of my robes. Then I can put your things in the dryer. They'll be ready in a jiffy."

That sounded reasonable. Better to dry her clothes here than to try to put on the dryer at home. Her parents might hear it. She had no intention of telling them about her spin through the rapids. She knew Alex would automatically keep the incident secret.

Jason directed her to his bedroom and went to prepare their hot drinks. The place was full of "stuff." There was a personal computer, a telescope, a TV hooked up to *two* VCR's and a compact disc player with wires leading to a couple of speakers that were each as big as her own chest-of-drawers.

Show me your platinum-plated charge card, why don't you?

Cindy had been in Jason's room before. They'd made out on his bed only last Tuesday. His many toys had never annoyed her before. Quite the opposite, she'd always seen them as evidence of a place she would someday like to reach. But now she was thinking of Bala's village, Mau Dogan, where you couldn't even take a bath without having to walk three miles. Bala was fascinated with Western society, but she couldn't imagine him ever having a room like this, even if he were to move to America and become fabulously wealthy. He might argue this point with her but he'd be wrong. There was a part of him she felt she knew better than he did. That part didn't need "stuff."

Cindy stripped off her clothes and dried herself with a towel she found in a drawer. Standing naked in Jason's room, she began to feel uneasy. She was tired and she was sore. Her exhilaration over being rescued had worn off. She didn't know what excitement Jason thought the night might still have in store. But had she been fresh, her uneasiness would probably have still been there. All of a sudden, Jason was the last person in the world she wanted to be with.

Something happened tonight that I'm missing.

The coolness of her feelings made no sense. Just

that morning she had steamed over the newspaper article; her loyalty had come instinctively. Why, on the drive to the park she'd told herself how lucky she was to have him as a boyfriend. What had happened between then and now? Was it Bala's heroic rescue? Maybe her feelings had not disappeared, just been redirected. No, that was not it. Her affection for Bala was a totally new thing. The way her heart had changed toward Jason had to do with Jason himself. Something he'd done, or something he'd neglected to do.

Something Karen might have missed, too?

The latter thought came as she caught sight of a photograph partially hidden in the corner behind a sweatshirt. Jason had quickly gone through his room before letting her in to change. Obviously, he had tried to hide the picture, but the shirt had fallen away. It was of him and Karen at the prom last year.

So he keeps her near his bed.

There was a robe in the closet she was able to tie tight enough at the waist that her breasts didn't pop out. Gathering together her soggy clothes, she returned to the game room. Jason was waiting for her. He took the clothes, disappeared for a couple of minutes, then reappeared with the hot chocolate. They sat together on the couch beside a pool table and a giant aquarium. Cindy let the cup warm her hands before taking a drink.

"I set the dryer to max," Jason said. "I hope you weren't wearing anything that can shrink."

"Just my underwear."

"I didn't see any underwear."

"Oh, I must not have been wearing any."

She had not intended to drop a suggestive remark. Jason brightened. "You're not wearing any this minute, that's for sure." He put down his cup, placed his hand on her shoulder. "You know, Cindy, you look very beautiful right now."

She took a gulp of the hot chocolate. The taste was too sweet. "I don't feel beautiful," she muttered.

His fingers played with the top of her arm. "How do you feel?"

"Tired. And grateful. I don't know how I'm ever going to repay Bala."

Jason glanced at the fish. "That was a nice jump he took off that hill," he agreed.

"It was absolutely awesome."

"But I think he made a mistake not letting me pluck you up from the tree." She did not respond. He added, "What did you think when you saw me up there?"

"I thought you looked like you were about to fall off."

Jason nodded gravely. "It wasn't the safest place in the world to be."

"Yeah."

He put his arm around her. "What's the matter, Cindy?"

"Nothing."

"You seem far away."

"I'm thinking."

"About what?"

"Nothing."

He forced a laugh. "All right, I understand. You don't want to talk. I don't want to, either."

He started to kiss her. With her fatigue, it was easier to cooperate than resist, although she was feeling about as romantic as she did when her seventy-year-old dentist cleaned her teeth.

But then Jason's kisses became insistent. He was pulling her down on the couch, tugging at the knot she had tied in the robe's belt. She snapped her head back. "No," she said.

His wide eyes were inches away. "Are you still shook from the fall in the water?"

"I—yes. I just want to rest here until my clothes are ready." She leaned her head into his chest. "OK?"

"Sure, whatever you want." He stroked her hair, which was not a particularly soothing thing to do with all the knots in it. "I don't know if I told you how relieved I was when you made it to the side safely."

"It was scary," she agreed.

His hand moved from her hair to her lower back, rubbing. "I don't know if I ever told you how important you are to me."

There's a lot of things you don't know if you've told me.

The sarcasm felt out of place in her own mind. She was glad Jason did not have ESP. "You don't have to say anything, Jason."

For a while he did as requested, and she began to doze. Her breathing deepened, developing a slight snoring sound, and she vaguely realized she was listening to herself falling asleep. That was fine; when she awoke her clothes would be dry and she would be able to get to her own bed.

But then, all of a sudden, Jason started kissing her again. These were hungry passionate kisses, never mind that her response was almost nonexistent. He yanked open the knot in the robe belt, running his hand up her side.

"Jason, stop, it's late."

"It's almost a new day," he said, excited, continuing to paw at her.

"But I'm tired."

He pulled at the top of her robe. "You're amazing."

"Jason."

"Come on, Cindy, don't be such a tease."

"Get off me!" she shouted, coming fully awake, sitting up forcefully and retying her robe. "Don't you ever call me a tease!"

There was blood in Jason's cheeks. "Well, what do you expect? You take off your clothes and put on that thing that doesn't hide a damn thing and you get all pissed that I start getting interested."

"I took off my clothes because they were wet, not because I was trying to get you excited. What do you think I am?"

Now he was mad. "I think you're just like all the other girls at school. You're all talk. You wiggle your ass in front of the whole city at the stadium to support the guys on the team, but in private you'd rather make it with some geek on the cross-country team who—"

Cindy slapped him across the face. An instant after she did so, she realized he couldn't have possibly been talking about her brother. He was referring to Ray, who used to go with Karen—

Something Karen missed— His temper?

Jason leapt to his feet and raised his arm to strike her, his handsome face almost unrecognizable because of his fury. Cindy made no move to protect herself. Or maybe she made the best move. She just stared him straight in the eye. Jason paused, then slammed his fist into his leg, turning away.

"You had no right to hit me," he said, disgusted, taking a deep breath.

"You had no right to say what you did."

He whirled. "What did I say!?"

She nodded slowly. "A lot. Enough." She stood. "I'm going to get my clothes."

"Cindy, wait, please!" He grabbed her by the shoulders, suddenly worried. "Look, I'm sorry. I apologize.

You know how much pressure I've been under lately?
I don't know why I said that. I don't feel that way."

He looked so totally miserable, her sympathy came
against her better judgment. "OK. We'll forget it. I
accept your apology. I'm sorry I slapped you."

Jason smiled. "So we're still friends?"

"Yeah. Sure."

They were great friends. When he took her home,
she couldn't remember ever feeling so glad to get out
of his car.

Alex pulled in the driveway while she was busy
unlocking the front door. He limped from the car to
the porch. His knee must be hurting. Her own ankle
wasn't exactly in bliss. They made a great pair. Except
Alex was smiling.

"How was Joni?" she asked, trying to sound upbeat
for his sake.

He sighed. "I think she's in love."

Cindy chuckled. "I get the feeling she's not the only
one. Did you kiss her good night?"

"Till our lips caught fire. How's your ankle? Bala
told us you'd bruised it."

They entered the house. Wolf must be still outside;
he usually came to greet her. Well, she wasn't going to
go looking for him now. "I'm fine. You didn't tell
Mom?"

"No."

"Good." She yawned. "I'm going to want to hear
every last detail about Joni's combustible lips tomorrow, but right now, I've got to go to bed."

Alex was sensitive to her unspoken moods. "But
you're OK?"

She nodded wearily. "I'm more than OK. I'm
Cindy Jones."

He surprised her with a tight hug. "Thank God I
didn't lose you tonight," he said.

"I knew you'd try to save me," she replied, squeezing him back, feeling her eyes burn. Then she laughed. "A pity you couldn't swim any better than me!"

Alex stepped back, grinned. "Ain't that the truth." He patted her on the side. "Sweet dreams, sis."

"You, too."

Cindy went to her room and lay down and fell into a sleep so deep she didn't remember dreaming at all. Alex had a different experience, though in the morning he was to recall nothing more than his sister. But for the time he dreamed, if it could be called that, he witnessed a scene so vivid and so awful that it seemed to scratch his very soul.

He was caught in the current of a warm river rushing toward a cliff. A blazing sun hung in a rusty sky. He could feel its heat in spite of being all wet. And he could hear a noise coming from the approaching cliff, not the sound of water crashing on hard rocks, but the cries of many animals, and maybe people, in terrible pain. As he listened, he realized that on the other side of the cliff was a thing whose nature it was to rip the life out of the living. How he knew this, he wasn't sure. But he was convinced if he didn't escape the river soon, he would come face to face with this thing, and that it would show him no mercy. He would become just another one of the victims whose death agony wailed in his ears.

He tried swimming for the sides of the river. The way was difficult and his time was short. Yet somehow he managed to reach the edge, only to discover that its walls were smooth, impossible to scale.

There never had been a way to escape. Everyone who entered the river was doomed to go over the edge. He had been born and he was going to die. He saw that the river flowed not with water, but with blood.

He began to panic. He began to cry for help. The sound of his pleas mingled with the sound of all those who had already taken the awful plunge. He would be one of them. It was his destiny.

Yet he did not fall when the river came to its end. He was instead lifted up into the air, where he floated on a hot dry draft. And then everything changed, and it could not be said to have changed for the better. The cliff remained, but the river vanished, and he himself was no longer the same. He could fly, and his path swooped him past the very base of the cliff. There he saw no people and heard no cries. He saw only animals, quick-footed and sharp-toothed predators, feeding on other animals that weren't so quick, or so cruel.

And he watched, feeling a great horror, because the feeding animals filled him with envy; the sight of the bloody carcasses were making him hungry.

Yes, he had changed.

CHAPTER

VIII

CINDY DIDN'T GO to school on Monday. Her ankle was still sore—she told her parents she had twisted it getting out of Jason's car—and she didn't want to be seen hobbling around on crutches. Fortunately, the foot was feeling much better on Tuesday.

On that particular morning, as she had done the previous Friday morning, she stepped out of her house early to collect the local paper, which was delivered twice weekly. There was another article by Kent Cooke starting on the second page, and she read it from beginning to end, standing in the cool sunlight at the end of her driveway.

KAREN HOLLY'S STRANGE GRIZZLY
By Kent Cooke

I received a lot of mail Saturday morning. Much of it was delivered to my office, not by the mailman, but by those who had written the letters. Apparently, a few people were concerned I might not hear their opinions in time to respond in today's edition. Not all the mail flattered my reporting abilities. Some of it was outright hostile. It was probably good that I'd decided to take Saturday off.

But the majority of the mail was encouraging. People were curious. They wanted to hear more. They wanted me to dig deeper. I must confess, I had anticipated their desires. Since my previous article probing into the unusual circumstances surrounding Karen Holly's death, I have been busy sniffing around. I hope I won't be accused of having purposely withheld information last week so that I could have more to talk about today. Practically everything I will relate today I learned early yesterday morning.

First I spoke to Lieutenant James Baker. He was the gentleman who arrived at the scene of Karen's death before anyone else, with, of course, the exception of Jason Whitfield. I had been trying to talk to the lieutenant for some time; it was only after my article appeared a few days ago that he consented to meet with me.

Lieutenant Baker seemed a troubled man, maybe even an angry one. But he wasn't angry at me or my work. The investigation into Karen's death was troubling him, too. Certain things didn't make sense, he said.

Rain had fallen the night of the tragedy, between the time Jason left Karen's body and the time the lieutenant reached the spot he had been directed to by Jason. In my hate mail many people said the rain was the reason there were no bear tracks. Lieutenant Baker dismissed this explanation. When he arrived at the top of Crystal Falls, he said the rain was nothing more than a light drizzle. It is true that within the hour, a heavy downpour was to start, but in the interlude the officer had plenty of time to scout the area. Even equipped with a special high-powered flashlight designed for police work, he found not a single bear track. Of course, as previously stated, he didn't find Karen's body, either, not until much later in the night, when he was returning to his car in the company of Deputy Jeff Pierce, walking along the lower level of Snake Tail River, miles from where Karen had supposedly met the grizzly.

Those who knew Karen personally will have to forgive what is said in the following paragraph. They may even want to skip it. Lieutenant Baker paled when discussing the matter. It has to do with the nature of Karen's head wound. The coroner's report stated, and I quote, "Her head had suffered from what appeared to be an extremely powerful blow—the top of the skull was cracked in several places."

The lieutenant didn't directly dispute the coroner's statement. But he did add something. When he pulled Karen from the river, he said, it looked as though her head had been grabbed by the ears and squashed together.

The only way I can imagine a grizzly creating this effect is if the animal had trounced on Karen's head while she was lying on the ground. It would be physically impossible that the damage was done by a single blow while she was standing or sitting. But, somehow, I can't see the bear jumping up and down on the poor dead girl, nor can I see the grizzly dragging her body to the river and tossing it in.

Lieutenant Baker wasn't worrying about his job when he told me these facts. He's leaving the Timber Police Force in a couple of weeks. He's moving to Los Angeles, where he plans to go into real estate. He says he no longer feels good about raising his kids in this town. The place is too dangerous.

Last week, when I mentioned a sledgehammer and a rake, I was implying they'd been previously planted in the vicinity, that the murder—if there was one—had been planned. But let's play pretend and let's keep things simple. Say we had someone who wanted to kill this girl. Say the desire to do so came to him on the spur of the moment, in a fit of anger perhaps. What can you kill a girl with in the mountains? Big rocks would be handy enough. And let's further imagine that this murderer, when he was done smacking Karen on the head, suddenly realized that he'd made a terrible mistake, that he was in big trouble. What could he do?

Maybe he could make it look like a grizzly attack. By getting a bigger rock, by getting a sharp branch, he could cave in her rib cage and tear her flesh and so mutilate her body that it would be hard to tell what had gotten her. Then, to further confuse the situation, he could carry her to the river and let her go over the falls.

Do I think Jason Whitfield killed Karen Holly? I keep asking that question, don't I? I'll tell you one thing, I don't think a grizzly did it.

The preliminary hearing into Karen's death is next Monday. My spies in the district attorney's office still say there isn't a chance Jason will go to trial. This strikes me as incredible considering the "reasonable doubt" any sane person must have about Jason's innocence. Why doesn't the state have access to the information I have? Could it be because Jason's father plays golf on Saturdays with people who represent the state?

What do I know, I'm just a hack reporter who's always dreaming up conspiracies.

I went to the game Friday night against Brea High. I'm a big football fan, as you're probably all aware, but the game was slow and sloppy even by my modest standards. Things got kind of interesting at halftime, though. A fight broke out between a player for Timber and a spectator. I don't know what the fight was about or how it got started. All I can say was that the player was Jason Whitfield, and that he yelled out a threat to kill one of his classmates.

That kid's got a hell of a temper.

The bell signaling the end of lunch had rung, and Cindy was walking across the courtyard with Pam before going to Miss Clemens's psychology class, when Bala stopped her. She had not seen him since she had fallen asleep in his arms. He looked worried.

"May I talk to you in private?" he asked her, glancing at Pam to indicate he also wanted her approval.

"Whatever Cindy talks about in private," Pam said, "I hear about on the phone that same night."

"Sure," Cindy said. "Pam, I'll catch up with you in a couple of minutes. OK?"

Pam nodded with exaggerated patience. "I suppose I must learn to deal with the rejection." Giving a theatrical swirl, she walked away.

"Did I offend her?" Bala asked.

"No," she said, not sure if he had. "She's always saying stuff like that." She smiled. "I was searching for you during lunch."

Bala glanced around. "Can we talk where there are fewer people?" he asked, serious.

"All right. Let's go sit on the stump."

This was the first time she didn't have to climb up the back of the tree. Bala simply lifted her onto the stump after leaping up himself. Settling herself, she could see the courtyard emptying quickly.

"What did you want to talk about?" she asked.

Bala withdrew the morning paper from his back pocket and her heart sunk in her chest. The article had been on her mind all morning. She hadn't talked to Jason about it yet. He didn't appear to have made it to school.

"Did you know this girl, Karen Holly?" Bala asked.

"Pam knew her better. She was Pam's cousin. Did you talk to her about the article?"

"I wanted to talk to you first."

"Why?"

"Because you are Jason's girlfriend."

She looked down. "What do you want to know?"

"How Karen died."

"A lot of people want to know that. Jason says a bear killed her."

"Do you believe him?"

She shrugged. "What else could it have been?"

"Cindy?" His hand touched her hand. His skin appeared so dark against hers. She must try to get more sun. "Do *you* believe him?" he repeated.

She looked into his big luminous eyes. "Why do you want to know?" she asked uneasily.

"It is important to me. I cannot explain why." He paused. "I cannot tell you all my reasons, at least. But when I read this"—he tapped the paper—"I was worried about you."

"I don't think I'll be spending much time alone with Jason from now on. You don't have to worry."

You could even try to take his place, if you wanted. I wouldn't stop you.

"Did something happen between you and him since last Friday?"

She ran her hands over her legs, glancing at the ground again. "Yes. It's a long story, and sort of private." She stopped. "We should be getting to class soon."

Bala was studying her. He was not the same person she thought she knew. He seemed confused. "How is your ankle?" he asked absently.

She wiggled it for his benefit. "Fine, thanks to you." She paused again, undecided whether she wanted to probe. "You have a lot on your mind?"

"The death of this young girl, particularly the way in which she died, disturbs me."

She nodded. "It's no fun reading about, that's for sure."

"Where is Jason today? I have not seen him."

"He may have taken the day off. You weren't thinking of asking him directly about Karen?"

"Yes, I was."

"That would be a bad idea, believe me. He hardly knows you, and I don't think you're one of his favorites."

"Does he have this bad temper the man in the paper mentioned?"

"He wouldn't kill anybody, if that's what you're asking."

"That *is* what I am asking," he replied, showing uncharacteristic impatience. He leaned close, gripping her arm. "Cindy, please? This is important."

"But *why?*"

"I cannot tell you why."

"And I can't tell you whether he did it or not!" she

shouted, the words out of her mouth before she realized. Bala let go of her arm and sat back.

"He could have?" he asked quietly.

She hung her head miserably. "I don't know." She sniffed. "I don't think so, but I don't know."

Why doesn't this death go away? Why does it hang around like it had a life of its own?

Bala thought about what she said for a moment. "How is Alex?" he asked suddenly.

"What?"

"Your brother? How is he doing?"

"Alex is fine."

"Good." He seemed on the verge of asking more, before deciding against it. He jumped off the stump, then helped her down, his massive hands practically encircling her narrow waist. His strength continued to amaze her.

If he wanted, he could snap me in two.

Where had that thought come from?

He let go of her. "You are different from any of the girls in my village," he said, staring down at her, his voice solemn, as though the difference were not something he necessarily would have wished for.

She forced a smile. "Because I have blond hair?"

He went to touch her hair, stopped himself with an effort. He nodded, averting his eyes. "That must be it, Cindy."

Cindy wasn't the only one in her family who was late to fifth period class that Tuesday afternoon. Alex had spent the entire lunch period looking for Joni, and had not found her. He had done the same thing the previous lunchtime, with the same result. He had ended up calling her house. Her aunt had answered. Joni was not feeling well, Mrs. Lee had said, and was resting in bed. Alex had been angry with himself for having kept her out so late Friday that she'd gotten sick. And now, with her second absence in a row, his disgust with himself had changed to concern for her. For some reason, Joni had struck him as the last person in the world who would get sick.

The second lunch bell had rung already, and the bulk of the school was busy expanding their minds with knowledge they would probably forget before the day was over. Alex put a quarter in the pay phone at the back of the gym, not ten steps from where he had skinned his knee during the race. Joni's aunt answered again.

"Mrs. Lee, this is Alex."

"Alex, how are you today?" She sounded happy to learn it was him, almost relieved. It had been the same the day before.

"I'm fine. How are you?"

"Wonderful." She was definitely exaggerating. "I suppose you're wondering why Joni hasn't been at school. The poor girl's still not herself."

"There is a bug going around." He hadn't actually heard of one in particular, but it seemed the thing to say. "What are her symptoms?"

The question stumped Mrs. Lee for a moment. "She just feels kind of lifeless, you know, like she can't do anything."

"Is she in bed now? I'd like to talk to her, if that would be all right."

The woman paused. "I'll check. Could you hold a moment?"

"Yes."

He waited two long minutes before Joni came on the line. There was a lifting and putting down of receivers. Joni was talking from a different phone.

"Alex?" Her voice was devoid of energy.

"Yeah, it's me. I've been worried about you. How are you doing?"

"Good."

"You don't sound so good. Do you have the flu or something?" He had to wait for an answer.

"I don't know."

He wondered if her problem might not be emotional, if the grief over the death of her parents might have resurfaced and knocked her whole system out of whack. "Are you drinking plenty of fluids?"

"Huh?"

"Have you been drinking orange juice and grape juice and stuff like that?"

"Yes, my aunt has juice in the house." She coughed, making a strange sound in her throat. "I'm glad you called, Alex."

"You know, I sat in on your biology class today and took a few notes. If you'd like, I could bring them by. You don't want to fall too far behind while you're out sick."

"No," she said quickly, her voice gaining a measure of life. "I don't want you to come over."

He tried to sound light. "I don't care if you're not looking as wonderful as usual. And I never get sick. I'm not worried about catching what you've got."

A faint note of humor entered her tone, and yet, strangely enough, it only served to deepen the gloom of the conversation. "What I've got isn't catching."

"Then there's no problem. I'll stop by after practice."

"No," she said again, anxious now. "I don't want to see you."

Alex felt a painful stab in his chest. The way they had kissed—she must care about him. "But why not?"

Joni's words descended to a faraway whisper. "My

aunt is here, but we don't really know each other. There's nothing between us. It's like I'm in an empty house. That's the way I want it right now." She coughed again, her vocal cords sounding as rough as sandpaper. "Stay away, Alex, just stay away."

He swallowed. "OK, if that's what you want."

They said their good-byes. Alex stood for a while holding the silent phone in his hand.

CHAPTER
IX

JONI HARPER WASN'T SEEN at school that week, but Jason Whitfield returned on Thursday. Cindy ran into him during the break between second and third periods. They made a date to have lunch together at the McDonald's a block away from the campus, or rather, Jason made the date. All through the morning Cindy wondered if she should use the time to tell him the romance was over. What made her hesitate was that she had still to figure out what had soured Jason in her mind. All she knew, for certain, was that her feelings for him had changed up at the waterfall, before he had gotten rough in his game room.

She had to wonder if Bala's song hadn't planted shamic seeds deep in her mind. The world looked different than it had the previous week. Pam's gossiping was no longer as interesting.

Jason took her to McDonald's on the back of his motorcycle. He drove fast, as usual, scaring her, and making a mess of her hair in the process. But he was kind enough to pay for her food. With his dad's money.

"You hear the game's on a Saturday this week?" he said when they were seated in a booth. He took a bite of his hamburger, reaching for his fries. A small box

115

of Chicken McNuggets and a carton of milk had made up her order. Her appetite was off.

"Yeah."

"We're playing Hope. They only lost twice last year. But I think we'll kick their butts, if we don't put the ball in the air more than half a dozen times. The game's at their stadium."

"So I heard."

"I hope I get the ball if the game's on the line like it was last week."

She opened her milk. "I don't see why they wouldn't trust you with it," she muttered.

He looked at her. "What's wrong?"

"Nothing."

"Are you still mad at me for Friday night?"

"No. I hardly remember it."

"Then what's bugging you?"

"Nothing. What time's your hearing on Monday?"

He stopped, with a french fry hanging out of the corner of his mouth. "Why do you bring that up?"

She shrugged. "I think it's more important to talk about that than the game. But if you don't want to, that's fine with me."

He began to chew slowly. "In a way, I'm glad you mentioned it. I might need some help from you. I was talking to my lawyer yesterday, and he said, after all the B.S. press this thing's been getting, it might not be a bad idea to have a few character witnesses present." He paused, adding, "He thought my current girlfriend would be a good one."

Cindy sighed. "I don't know, Jason."

"What don't you know?"

I don't know if you're a good one.

"I have school on Monday."

His tone sharpened. "So what's one day of school? My ass is on the line."

116

"I heard the hearing was just a formality."

"Who told you that?"

"You did."

He was annoyed. "It was, last week. But with that jerk's articles, the D.A.'s going to have to act like he's hot on my tail."

"He's just going to act?"

Jason did a double take. "He's going to do his job," he said carefully. "Will you help me, Cindy?"

She almost told him, right then, that it was finished between them. What stopped her was a peculiar intuition that there might be a value in attending the hearing, a value outside of what Jason was counting on. Analyzing the feeling, she failed to find the rationale behind it.

"Can I think about it?" she said.

"Sure. Can I have my lawyer call you?"

"Sure."

Hope High's cross-country course was a piece of cake next to Timber's. It was also unimaginative and boring. There was a fine park adjoining the school, but they'd chosen to construct a route completely within the campus, using the track, various playing fields and an assortment of loops through the buildings. By squeezing a three-mile course into a school that could hold less than a thousand students, they'd created a situation where the runners had to cover the same ground again and again. Alex didn't care. There were no hills. He hated hills.

As usual, Cindy and Pam were there to cheer for him. Alex wished Joni had been able to come. Here it was Friday and she still hadn't returned to school. He was going to call her after the race, he'd decided, and he was going to go see her no matter how much she felt she needed to be alone. The more he'd thought of

it, the more obvious it'd become she was depressed.
She needed a friend. She needed him. He would call
her after he won.

The hunted, the hunter.

They had removed their sweats and were walking
over to the starting line. Cindy had just given him a
good-luck kiss and Pam had just kicked Ray in the
shins. Alex was surprised at his lack of tension. He'd
lost last week and still his confidence was high. He
kept thinking about how it'd been on the couch with
Joni, how her mouth had seemed to almost swallow
him. That had been nice.

"Going to trip over any cheerleaders this week,
Alex?" Ray asked in his usual jovial way.

"Only if they throw themselves at my feet. Going to
remember to tie your shoes?"

"Damn, I shouldn't have quit Boy Scouts when I
did." Ray laughed, kneeling to take care of his laces.
They had both been loose. Alex waited for him
patiently, reflecting that Ray and he had not talked
once about Joni all week.

"Hurry," he said after a minute. "Their coach is
loading the starting pistol."

Ray stood, brushing off his chubby knees. "What
kind of pace are you going to set, buddy?"

"A merciless one," Alex lied.

He was taking Joni's advice. When the gun went off,
he didn't rush to the front. He tucked in behind Ray,
who was in turn following a short redhead whom Alex
knew to be Hope's strongest runner. He had barely
defeated the guy last year.

They circled the track twice, then headed onto the
baseball field. The grass under their feet was thick and
made for a slow surface. Alex didn't mind. He had
fallen into an excellent rhythm. This lagging behind
wasn't so bad. He realized he'd always been afraid to

use this tactic before because of his lack of confidence. He'd always been so afraid of losing that he'd felt he had to win every blessed yard of every course. In reality, with his kick, it made sense to take it easy at the beginning. Joni had taught him more in a minute than his coach had in three years.

Alex thought of Joni as he ran. He would buy flowers before he visited her. Roses, yeah, what girl didn't like roses? The thing was, he had to get her out of that house, away from her aunt. The woman was nice enough but it was a fact it had also been her sister who had died. How could being around Mrs. Lee not help but depress Joni?

As they entered the third mile, Alex knew he was in good shape. The redhead had led most of the way, with Ray occasionally pressing the pace. Alex had allowed them a thirty-yard lead, but now he began to close that gap. With a half a mile to go, he drew even, noting with pleasure how hard his two opponents were breathing. His own breathing was heavy but didn't feel strained. He remembered the speed the redhead had showed in the final stretch last year. Feeling how much spring he had in his own legs, he wasn't worried.

Ray charged to the lead as they reentered the track. The Hope runner hung close and Alex stayed on his heels. He could hear Cindy shouting his name. The fatigue was there, but he had it under control. He switched to his reserves and found them waiting to be used. Half a lap from the finish, he accelerated in a burst, passing the others. He knew he had it at that point. But hitting the tape a few seconds later still felt divine.

Ray finished third. Sweating like a bear, he gave him a congratulatory hug as they exited the chute. "Nice kick at the end, Alex," he gasped. "If only I'd had my doughnuts this week, I might have made it closer."

Alex smiled. "Fast on them for the next week and you'll be back on top." It was easy to be the nice guy when you were a winner. He let his head fall back, drinking up the air, tasting the sweetness of victory. For the rest of the season, he swore, he was going to enjoy this sensation after every race.

"Alex!"

Cindy was as happy, if not more so, than he was. One of the main reasons he always wanted to win so badly was to give her something to cheer about. She squeezed him tightly, not minding the fact she was staining her song uniform with his sweat. "You were magnificent!" she said.

"You stunk," Pam told Ray, who had bent back over, trying to catch his breath. "You choked. Alex stomped your ass. You should quit while you're only third rate."

Ray smiled, letting himself fall over onto his butt on the ground. "I love you, too, baby."

Alex came back to earth hard and quick after they'd showered and were walking to the bus for the ride home. He was alone with Ray. They'd changed quickly and were ahead of the others. Alex spotted a phone attached to Hope's administration building. He went to excuse himself.

"Who are you calling?" Ray asked.

He saw no point in lying. "Joni Harper. You must have noticed she hasn't been in this week. I think she's going through a rough time."

"She sounded all right to me."

Alex stopped in midstride, glancing back at him. "When did you talk to her?"

"Yesterday."

"But she wasn't at school yesterday."

Ray shrugged. "We talked on the phone."

Alex's heart skipped a beat. "You called her? When did you get her number?"

"We exchanged numbers the first week of school. But I didn't call her. She called me."

"*What?* Why would she call you?"

Ray couldn't understand his amazement. "I'm her friend. Maybe she was bored. She wanted to know if I wanted to do something this weekend."

Alex went very still. He had not calmed down. He had gone into mild shock. "What did you tell her?"

Ray was beginning to realize this wasn't a casual situation. "I told her, sure," he said slowly. "I didn't think it was any big deal."

Alex had to fight to keep his voice from trembling. "But you knew I was going out with her. You saw us together at the game, for god's sakes."

"What of it? You went out on a date. You didn't exchange vows."

"It wasn't just a date. We— How can she go out with you? She's sick."

"Like I said, she sounded all right on the phone." Ray paused, ran his hand through his hair. "You're not mad, are you?"

Alex looked away. She told him to stay away. Then she had called Ray. Lord, *she* had asked Ray out! This did not make sense. She cared about him. She had made that clear. They had held hands and kissed and made plans to do things together.

But maybe she would just as easily do all those things with Ray. Maybe she would do even more with him.

"Just once I've got to know what that soft white skin feels like under my fingers."

"I'm not happy about it," he said quietly.

Ray looked uncomfortable. "Hey, that's your own fault if you're not. I told you earlier I was going to hit on her. You didn't tell me not to."

Alex considered a move he had sworn he would never take. "And what if I told you now?"

Ray took a step back, folded his arms across his chest. "I can't do that, Alex."

He raised his voice. "Why not?"

"I told her I'd go out with her. I hate going back on my word."

"Your *word?* You're stabbing an old friend in the back, and you're worried about your word to a girl you hardly know?"

Ray was insulted. "I'm not stabbing you in the back."

"Have you got another name for taking a guy's girl?"

"She's not your girl. If she was, she wouldn't be going out with me. She wouldn't have *asked* me out."

"I don't believe she did ask you out. I think you just weaseled her into doing something she doesn't really want to do!"

Ray's tone sharpened. "Call her."

"Why should I call her?"

"To ask her what I weaseled her into. Go ahead, there's a phone. What are you afraid of?"

That she'll hang up on me.

Alex shook his head, the fight suddenly going out of him. "I'm not going to call her," he muttered.

Ray also softened. "I'm sorry, Alex. I guess I did know you liked her. But I couldn't resist."

"It's that hard?" he asked wearily. Stupid question; who knew better than he how hard it was not to want Joni Harper.

Ray appeared thoughtful, even perplexed. He stared at a group of young children who were playing on a swing in the park across the street. "I don't know what it is. I told you I'm going to try to get back with Pam? Right after the race, I asked her if she wanted me to drop by Sunday afternoon. She just laughed at me. But I know she meant, yes. I miss Pam, you know? I really do. But I feel I've just got to go out with Joni this one time."

"You're not making sense."

Ray glanced his way, trying to smile. "I told you before, it's like she's cast a spell on me. She's called and I have to follow." He put his hand on Alex's shoulder, spoke seriously. "It'll just be this once. And nothing will happen, buddy, I promise."

He nodded. "All right, Ray, whatever you say."

Alex ended up driving back to Timber in the car with Cindy. He did not take the bus. He never saw Ray alive again.

123

CHAPTER
X

CINDY WAS DOING the laundry when the reporter Kent Cooke came to the door. With the hours her parents put in at the store, there wasn't much time left over for them to take care of household chores; for that reason, Cindy didn't mind washing the dirty clothes. Normally, she took care of them Sunday night; but with Jason's hearing, she'd decided to take Monday off, and had postponed the chore until Monday morning. Jason's lawyer had called her Saturday afternoon, and that cat sure had been persuasive. He should've been a used-car salesman. He'd not only tried to convince her to appear as a character witness, he'd tried to program her as to exactly what she was supposed to say. But she had a mind of her own. She might just stay home all day.

Jason's the most thoughtful and sensitive boy I know. He has never once tried to take advantage of me nor has he ever raised his voice in my presence—Come on, give me a break. He's as horny and as loud as any guy I know.

At the knock at the door, Wolf rushed to her side and Sybil said hello to Joni. That stupid bird really had taken a liking to Alex's friend. Sybil had been calling for Joni for the last week.

"Cindy," Cindy said as she swept past the bird cage. "Hello, Cindy Jones."

"Hello, Joni Jones."

"Dumb, dumb," Cindy muttered.

"Hello, Dumb Jones."

The newspaper always ran a miniature black and white of Kent Cooke at the top of his column. As a result, Cindy recognized the man instantly. That didn't lessen her surprise.

"Can I help you?" she asked warily, standing with the door only partway open. He had to be close to forty, but there was something in his face and the way he held himself that made him seem younger. His big ears would have done better with a thicker head of hair, and his sports coat needed pressing.

"Are you Cindy Jones?"

"Yes."

"Do you know who I am?"

"You write for the paper."

He nodded. "I'm Kent Cooke, yes. May I come in?"

She hesitated. "I'll be off to school in a few minutes."

He consulted his watch. "Are you sure you're going today, Cindy? You're already late."

"What do you want?"

"If I may come in and have a seat, I'll tell you."

"All right." She opened the door all the way. Wolf sniffed the man's hand, and Mr. Cooke patted the dog on the head, making himself comfortable on the couch. Cindy sat on the edge of a chair directly across from him. "Go on," she said.

He smiled briefly. "You don't seem overjoyed to see me, Cindy. Have you read my articles about Karen Holly and Jason Whitfield?"

"I've seen them."

"I understand you're Jason's latest girlfriend?"

"We're friends," she said cautiously. Mr. Cooke noted her tone.

"I hear you're going to appear at his hearing today as a character witness?"

"Who told you that?"

He shrugged. "Reporters have to protect their sources. And does it matter? Are you going to the hearing?"

"I might."

"What are you going to say? If you go, that is?"

"Are you going to be there, Mr. Cooke?"

"Certainly."

"Then you'll find out then."

He leaned forward, studied her. "Let's not fence with each other. You're Jason's girl, and he can't have helped give you a favorable impression of me. He's probably told you I'm on his case just so I can make his father, the mayor, look bad."

"I form my own opinions of people, Mr. Cooke. What is it you want?"

He sat up. "The truth. I want to know whether Jason killed Karen. I would want to know this no matter whose son he was."

"Why don't you let the police and the courts decide if he killed her?"

"If they were free to go about this investigation in a normal fashion, I would. But they're not; they're being obstructed. Before you dismiss this possibility, let me tell you who appoints the sheriff in this town—Jason's father. It's Timber's sheriff who's been overseeing the investigation since the night Karen died. And things have not been going by the book. Karen's own parents have been unable to obtain a full report of the autopsy. That alone would indicate that outside 'influences' are at work."

"What does any of this have to do with me? Do you want me to take the stand today and tell the judge that Jason has tried to kill me a couple of times?"

He stared at her a moment. "Has he?"

"No! What kind of question is that?"

Mr. Cooke paused. "As I mentioned in my article, I went to the game a week ago last Friday. I saw Jason fighting with Ray Bower. I saw you trying to break up that fight. I heard threats shouted."

"It was just a silly argument. It was nothing serious."

Mr. Cooke shook his head sadly. "I'm afraid it's very serious, Cindy. How well did you know Ray?"

Her heart began to pound silently. "I've known him a long time. Since I was a kid. Why?"

"Then I'm sorry I'm the one who has to bring you this news." He cleared his throat. "Ray's dead."

She almost laughed, the remark sounded so absurd. Ray couldn't be dead; he'd just run against her brother on Friday and he'd never looked more alive. *What?*

"The police found his body at three this morning at the national park, though it appears he'd been dead at least twenty-four hours. Apparently, he went out with a girl Saturday night. He dropped her off about eleven but never made it home."

Cindy closed her eyes, moaning inside. All those great gross jokes, those loud obnoxious laughs—no more. "How did it happen?" she whispered.

"Whatever or whoever got hold of Karen appears to have gotten hold of Ray. In fact, the officer I spoke to said Ray's body was in worse shape." He added, "It was difficult to make the identification."

"A grizzly," she mumbled.

"It was no grizzly, Cindy. Ray was murdered. He

was murdered by the same person who murdered Karen."

"But what does the girl say? My brother said Ray was going out with Joni Harper."

"She doesn't know anything."

"But isn't she a suspect?"

"Joni Harper is a ninety-nine pound seventeen-year-old."

"But Jason couldn't have done this. How could he have? If what you say is true, he wouldn't have had the strength."

"I know this is not easy. I hate talking about it. But since we must, if you think about it, once Jason had Ray unconscious, or dead, he could, with suitable tools, do just about anything he wanted to his body."

Cindy bent over, her stomach heaving. "No!" she cried. "Jason would have no motive."

"An angry man doesn't need a motive. Outside of his anger. He'll do anything."

"You're saying Jason's a psychotic? Is that what you're saying?"

"Yes."

Cindy sat upright, put her arm over her eyes. "I want you to leave."

"I will, in a moment. But first I want to ask you something. Has Jason ever given you a hint of being badly disturbed?"

"No," she said flatly. Alex would have no one to run against. Pam would have no one to make fun of. . . .

"Are you sure?"

"Yes. Now please, go."

"But surely you've seen signs of his temper?"

She grabbed the arms of the chair, glaring. "So what? Lots of people have tempers. That doesn't mean they cut people up. Do you think I would've gone out with him if I thought he might kill me? Why,

just last week we were up at the mountains and he—"
She stopped.

Tried to save my life? Why did my life need saving?
Kent Cooke was watching her intently. "Please
continue, Cindy."

"It was nothing," she muttered, thinking. Jason had
dragged her up to Castle Park. He had dragged the
whole group up there. And he'd insisted they go to a
cave, a cave Alex thought didn't even exist.

"But you were saying you were up at the mountains
and Jason did something. What did he do?"

"Nothing," she said evenly. "He didn't do a damn
thing."

Mr. Cooke stood reluctantly, sighing. "It's a terrible
thing that happen to Karen. It's even worse that it had
to happen to Ray, too. I hope this is the end of it. I
pray that it is. But frankly, I'm worried it's not.
Jason's lying. If he had nothing to hide, he'd be telling
the truth. His hearing is in five hours. I've already
learned that Ray's death will not be brought into the
proceedings. Don't ask me why not. The D.A. doesn't
even have anyone lined up to question Jason's story.
But Jason's lawyer has you scheduled. Think about it,
Cindy, would you? I've been watching you. Each time
I've mentioned Jason's name, even before I told you
about Ray, you didn't react like a girl who didn't have
doubts. A lot depends on you. Up on the stand, you
might be the only voice Karen and Ray have got."

Cindy stood, composing herself, gesturing toward
the door. "I can't talk anymore. I have things I have to
do."

He nodded sympathetically. "You strike me as an
intelligent young lady. I know you'll carefully consider the situation. See you at the hearing." He opened
the door, took a step outside. "Once again, I'm sorry I
had to be the bearer of bad tidings."

"So am I," she said softly.

When Mr. Cooke was gone, Cindy began to make plans. Alex had taken the car to school. He'd said he'd call at lunch to see if she still wanted to go to the hearing, which was in Cheyenne, two hours away. She could call the school now and have him return home immediately, but then she'd probably have to be the one to break the bad news. It appeared the reporter was several steps ahead of the general public when it came to local news. It was her responsibility to try to console Alex, she knew, but if she got involved in that at the moment she'd lose the time between now and the hearing. And if she called her parents at the store, they'd ask too many questions and probably not let her out of the house for fear she might drive into a tree or something in her distressed state.

There was really only one choice. She'd have to take her dad's seldom used motorbike sitting in the garage. She'd only had a couple of lessons on the thing. Jason had given them to her.

Cindy put on a leather jacket she never wore and stuffed a Polaroid in the inside pocket. Outside, the bike started up without a hitch. In a way she might be better off with it than a car. She should be able to run the cycle pretty far up Pathfinders Trail.

Alex didn't learn of Ray's death until snacktime, between second and third periods. He was hanging out near the science building, talking to Bala. It had been Bala who had started the conversation. He seemed sort of down and Alex could relate to that; Alex had spent the entire weekend dialing Joni's number on an unplugged phone.

But I didn't really call her. If she can call Ray, she can call me.

Bala seemed to be having girl troubles of his own.

He was asking about Cindy and Jason, how close they really were. Looked like Superman was falling for his sister. At least, that's what Alex thought was going on. Bala was beating around the bush. He also kept bringing up Joni, maybe trying to impress upon him that their situations were very similar.

"Just a minute, Bala," Alex interrupted. "I'm the last person who can give you advice. Believe me, I don't understand a thing about women. And that includes my sister."

Bala appeared taken aback. "I am not asking your advice, Alex, although I would welcome it if the situation called for it. What I am seeking, without wishing to pry, is information."

Alex felt Bala was just too embarrassed to come right out and say he had the hots for Cindy. Alex was somewhat relieved to see these problems were international in scope. "Ask me something specific. Then maybe we can make some progress."

"How well does Cindy know Jason?"

"Pretty well."

"Would she try to protect him?"

"Are you referring to his hearing? You don't have to worry about that. Jason didn't kill Karen. All this talk going around is just hot air. A bear got that girl."

"How can you be sure?"

Alex shrugged. "What else could it have been? Anyway, I thought you wanted to know about Cindy? Look, I'll tell you what I'll do. Next time I see her, I'll bring you up and see how she reacts. This will be between you and me."

Bala frowned. "Why would you do this?"

Alex smiled. "Bala, you like her, admit it. You may as well find out if she likes you."

Bala turned away. "It is true I find your sister an extraordinary human being."

"Extraordinary human being—that's a great way to put it. I'll have to remember that when I think of Joni."

Bala eyed him. "How do you feel when you are with Joni?"

"On our date I felt fine. Better than fine. But now I'm wondering where it all went. How do you feel when you're with Cindy?"

Bala didn't seem to hear the question. "Did you ever feel uneasy?"

Alex blushed. "Well, there were a few moments, here and there, you know?"

"Tell me."

"I shouldn't be talking about these things."

"Did you feel scared when her body touched yours?"

"Hey, now hold on! I'm not saying we did anything."

Bala was insistent. "Did her mouth touch yours?"

"Bala, listen, in our society you don't ask people of integrity questions like that. Sure, I kissed her good night. We don't have to go into how much anatomy was involved."

"And you did not feel scared?"

Alex sighed. "How did all this get started?"

Bala's brow was furrowed in concentration. "If it were so, there would be signs," he muttered to himself.

"Huh?"

"Alex, have you been having any dreams? Nightmares about awful bloody things?"

Alex shook his head, getting more confused by the moment. "And I thought I was going through a rough time with Joni. Look, Bala, Cindy is easy to get to know. All you've got to do is—"

Alex spotted Pam at that instant. He almost didn't

recognize her. Pam wasn't the prettiest of girls, but she usually had a spark to her. Such was not the case now. She was weaving like a drunk, apparently searching for someone she couldn't find. Bala saw her, too. They hurried to her side.

"Pam, is something wrong?" Bala asked, concerned. Pam took a moment to recognize him. Tear stains dampened her cheeks. Bala grabbed her by the shoulders, shook her gently. "Pam?"

"Bala, I'm looking for Cindy. I need a ride home."

"Why do you need a ride?" Bala asked.

Pam looked down, squinted her eyes as though something irritating had lodged in them. "Because my head is screwed up. I don't think I can drive."

"Why do you have to go home?" Alex asked.

Pam gazed at him in wonder. "Alex, do you know where Cindy is?"

Pam phasing in and out like this was unbelievable. She was usually as steady as a rock. "Never mind, Cindy," Alex said. "We can give you a ride. Tell us what's wrong?"

"It's Ray," she said. Then her whole face crumbled and she began to cry. "He's dead."

"Ray's dead?" Alex said in disbelief. "No, he's fine. What are you talking about?"

Pam continued to sob and it was only Bala who was keeping her on her feet. "My mother called the school," she said. "She wants me to come home. Something killed Ray."

"What?" Bala asked sharply.

Pam sniffed. "They think it was Mr. Bear. He got Karen and now he's gotten Ray."

"Mr. Bear?" Alex chuckled, though he felt far from happy. "Pam, what exactly did your mother say?"

Exasperation pierced through her grief. It appeared to help her get a grip on reality. "She said Ray was dead! What else do you want to hear? Some animal got hold of him. Now just shut up and take me home!" Her face fell on Bala's chest. "Damn this world," she moaned.

Bala backed away from Pam slowly. Alex had to move to support her. Bala's face had undergone a complete metamorphosis. His aura of quiet strength had disintegrated. Pure cold horror had replaced it. So frightening was the change in him, Alex didn't even have a chance to assimilate that Ray really was gone.

"Bala, what is it?"

"It is true," he whispered. "What I was told is true."

"What's true? What's going on? Do you know what has happened to Ray?"

Bala turned away, leaning his head on the wall of the science building. "I was warned."

Alex was having to fight too many things at once. Pam was collapsing in his arms. Bala was mumbling gibberish. "Who warned you about what?"

"My grandfather warned me about the girl."

"Bala, I need some help here. We've got to get Pam home. We can talk on the way." Alex winced. "God, I hope none of this is really happening."

Bala stood abruptly upright, turning toward them, trying to master himself. "Alex, you told me Ray went out with Joni last Saturday?"

"Yes."

Pam broke suddenly from his arms, spoke savagely, "I'm going to find Cindy. You guys don't know what's happening." She began to hurry away. Alex moved to follow.

"Cindy's not at school today," he called. Bala grabbed his arm.

"You're going to have to take Pam home."

"Fine, let go of me and I'll do just that," Alex said, shaking loose.

"Give me the keys to your car first," Bala said, blocking his way.

"Why?"

"I will explain later."

Alex removed them from his pocket and Bala snatched them up. "Do you know how to drive?" Alex asked.

"I have watched Pam do it. Listen to me, Alex, I have something important to tell you. Do not call Joni to ask what happened to Ray."

That was exactly what he'd planned to do. "Why shouldn't I? She might know something."

Bala's voice was urgent. "That does not matter. What I have to say does. Have no contact with her whatsoever. Do not talk to her. If she should call you, hang up the phone. And do not go see her. Alex, a dozen times you have said you did not know how to thank me for saving your sister's life. This is how you can thank me. By doing what I say and not asking me why you should do it."

"But this could be a terrible trauma for Joni. She might be distraught, and need my help."

Bala closed his eyes for a second and took a hissing breath. "Joni is not distraught. That would not be possible."

"Bala—?"

"I have said too much. I have stalled too long. Go to Pam, take care of her." He gave Alex a quick hug, a sad note entering his tone. "Perhaps some time you can ask Cindy about me. Another time, perhaps."

He sounds like he thinks he's going to die, too.

Alex wasn't given the opportunity to ask if that

were true. Bala, running at a pace Alex could never have matched, disappeared in the direction of the parking lot.

Cindy was fortunate. The motorbike got her to within a mile of the top of Crystal Falls. But while racing up the trail, she'd almost flattened a ranger on foot. She was worried he might try to write her a ticket on the way back, or worse, confiscate her bike. For that reason, when the path suddenly hit a rocky step that was meant to be tackled by carefully placed feet, she hid the cycle off the path behind a bush.

It was only eleven. The point where she had entered the water was an hour away, maybe less if she could jog part of the way. She should be able to get up and down in time to make the hearing.

Depending on how long it takes to get rid of my paranoia.

That was the problem. She didn't know what she was looking for. Perhaps she should have invited Kent Cooke. If nothing else, that guy didn't miss much. Five minutes talking to her and he'd known she didn't trust Jason.

Hurrying up the trail, panting on the crisp forest air, she thought of Ray—not of anything specific they'd done together, or of anything in particular he had said—she just thought of his face, and his laugh. It seemed to give her strength.

When she reached the place where Wolf had tried to eat Jason, where the falls tumbled into the wide churning bowl two hundred feet below, she decided on a short detour. The quickest route to the narrow path that led to Jason's supposed cave was to cut between the loop of the river. But she chose to stay close to the water. She wanted a look at that tree Jason had been hanging from.

The current wasn't quite as strong as when she'd gone for her swim. Nevertheless, rainstorms farther back in the mountains must be continuing to stock the river; the level was considerably higher than it normally was at that time of year.

She hesitated as she stepped onto the overhanging log. If she went in now, there would be no apprentice sorcerer to pluck her out. What finally gave her the courage to proceed was the sight of a short piece of rope sticking out from close to the spot Jason had been. Going down on all fours, she crept toward it.

Initially, a closer view didn't tell her much. It was rope, maybe even from her parents hardware store, and it appeared to have been cut at both ends by a sharp knife. The only surprise was that a gust of wind hadn't knocked it into the water; it wasn't attached to anything.

Not now at least.

Leaning forward, she noticed there were friction marks on the thick branch Jason had been hanging from. They'd been created by a larger piece of rope, wrapped several times around the branch, under pressure. That was very interesting. She pulled out her camera and took a picture.

The branch had been fortified to keep it from breaking.

Cindy used more film when she reached the spot where her trusty basketball shoes had failed her. What was left of the branch she had grabbed at the start of her ordeal had been cut—by a sharp knife, probably —from underneath, over three quarters of the way through. In other words, it had been left in place as a false reassurance of safety.

But it was the ground that made her realize beyond a shadow of a doubt that her deepest fears were true. Going down on her knees, brushing aside the gravel that had been hurriedly thrown over this portion of the path, she gathered together a slimy substance that rolled with calculated smoothness between her trembling fingers.

Someone had previously oiled the spot.

Nothing was making sense. When Alex finally got Pam home, and the girl had finished exchanging a tearful hug with her mother, disappearing into her bedroom where her sobs could still be heard coming through the walls, Alex learned from Mrs. Alta that Bala had just been there.

"But he insisted I take Pam home because he had something he had to do right away," Alex said. He desperately needed a moment to himself where he could let the grief—and, yes, guilt—over Ray's death come to the surface. Choking it back inside, he felt ready to burst.

"He was here two minutes when he was back out again," Mrs. Alta said, nervously rearranging the apples and bananas in the fruit bowl for no apparent purpose. A homely, older version of Pam, she had known Ray as long as any of them. "He didn't even turn off his car."

"That was my car." Alex rubbed his head, trying to assemble all the bizarre things Bala had said into a meaningful framework. Something about a warning that had been true about a girl. Then he had started on him to stay away from Joni. Was she this girl? "Mrs. Alta, what did he do when he was here?"

"Nothing that I know of. Except that he took a blanket when he left." She wiped at her eyes. "I don't know if I should call Ray's mother or wait for a couple of days. That poor woman."

"A blanket? That's weird. Wait a second. Could he have been carrying something in this blanket?"

"I don't know. I've never seen Bala so anxious. He's always so calm. I didn't think he knew Ray at all."

"He only knew him in passing. Can you remember anything, anything at all, he did besides grab the blanket?"

"Well, he went into the basement. But just for a minute."

That was not what Alex wanted to hear. He knew Pam's dad was a greater gun enthusiast than his own father, and that he kept his rifles and pistols downstairs in a locked cabinet. Alex quickly excused himself.

"Joni is not distraught."

The basement was gloomy. Alex didn't need the lights on, however. Bala's haste was again in evidence. There was glass on the floor, from where he had smashed into the cabinet. Mr. Alta had a collection of fine handguns, six of them to be exact, each with its own special place. One of the places was empty.

Alex took four steps at a time going back up the stairs.

"Mrs. Alta, may I use your phone? Thank you, I've got to make a call." Alex punched out Joni's number from memory. Joni's aunt answered.

"Hello?"

"Hi, Mrs. Lee. Is Joni there?"

"Alex?"

"Yes, it's me. I must speak to Joni immediately."

"She's not here."

"Where is she?"

"That tall African boy came over. They went out together."

"In the neighborhood?"

"Well, they took the car. It looked like your car."

"It is," Alex muttered, leaning against the wall, a weakening despair rising up his legs into his chest.

Bala had gone off the deep end. He blamed Joni for Ray's death. And he was carrying a gun.

"I'm glad you called, Alex. A lot has been going on. The police were over earlier asking Joni about the boy she went out with Saturday night. I understand he hadn't been back home. That's what Joni told me, at least. Then this black fellow came by." Her voice lowered, becoming confidential. "Between the two of us, I don't much care for her being around that sort. She's had trouble with them in the past."

Alex's ears perked up. "What sort of trouble?"

"It was a long time ago," Mrs. Lee said reluctantly. "I'd rather not discuss it now." Her tone brightened. "At least Joni's feeling better. She woke up Sunday morning looking wonderful."

"I'm happy to hear that, Mrs. Lee," Alex said. "Are you going to be there? I think I should come over."

There were few people at the courthouse. Cindy was surprised. She'd figured, with all the publicity, the curiosity seekers would be out in droves. Then again, this was a hearing, not a trial. And Timber and Cheyenne weren't exactly next-door neighbors.

She was hanging out near the courtroom Jason's lawyer had told her about on the phone when the lawyer suddenly appeared through the doors. He had a large black moustache and pale brown eyes. The smoothness in his voice sounded phony.

"Cindy, I'm Michael Kenner. I'm glad to see you could make it."

"Am I late?" The hike back to the bike had taken longer than anticipated. Her discovery had worn her out. All the times she'd spent alone with Jason, kissing him, talking with him about her future, kept crowding uncomfortably into her mind. All those times he hadn't given a damn about her.

The lawyer smiled. "The hearing has been on for a while but they've only been covering material that wouldn't be of interest to you." He took her by the arm. "I'll be calling you to the stand soon. Do you remember what to say?"

"Yes. I have a good memory."

"Just keep it short. Answer my questions as I give them to you. It's not necessary to go overboard praising Jason."

Cindy forced a laugh. "Oh, I won't do that."

The lawyer settled her into a wooden pew several rows behind Jason. Her "boyfriend" turned and gave her a wink. She smiled, and he would have shook in his seat if he had known what was behind that smile. On the other side of the room, she spotted Kent Cooke. He, too, noted her arrival. He held her eye for a moment before turning back to listen to the proceedings.

The district attorney, a short elderly man of Japanese descent, was questioning Timber's sheriff. Cindy half listened. They were probably all lying.

Jason's lawyer called her to the stand not long after. They gave her a Bible to put her hand on and she swore to tell the whole truth and nothing but. The judge leaned her way from his position behind his high desk. He had the shiniest head of silver hair she had ever seen.

"Miss Jones, how long have you known Jason Whitfield?" the lawyer asked as he paced confidently in front of her.

"I've known him casually since I entered Timber High three and a half years ago. We've only been dating seriously for the last four weeks."

"In this four-week period, how often have you seen Jason?"

"Almost every day."

"So we could safely say you know him well?"

Cindy glanced at Jason. He nodded to let her know she was doing a good job. "I feel like I know him better than his parents do." Then before the lawyer could ask another question, she said, "I'd like to relate a story that tells just what kind of guy he is. It'll only take a few minutes."

The lawyer glanced at her in surprise, though without alarm. Cindy turned to the judge, who appeared to check with the lawyer, and then shrugged. "Please go on, Miss Jones," the judge said.

In a concise methodical fashion, she told the court about the hike up to Crystal Falls, starting with Jason's suggestion in the parking lot at lunch, and ending with Jason's criticism of Bala's tactic in rescuing her. It was at this point Jason's lawyer interrupted. He'd been dying to do so since she'd told of falling in the water.

"This is all very interesting, Miss Jones, and I'm sure you had a night you'll not soon forget. But the fact that Jason was unable to rescue you, despite making a valiant attempt, isn't of direct relevance to the issue at hand."

"But it is," she said. "What went on that night could explain why Karen Holly died."

Jason began to fidget. His lawyer lost his pleasant smile. "Really, Miss Jones, we know why Karen Holly died and we have had numerous testimony by experts to that effect. Now if you will just—"

"I have to finish my story," she said quickly, appealing to the judge. The man raised his eyebrow.

"There's more?"

"Yes, your honor. This morning I went back up to the place where I almost drowned. I made a few discoveries. First, the branch Jason had been hanging from had been supported by a rope. Second, the branch I grabbed when I was falling had previously been doctored so that it couldn't possibly support my weight. Third, someone had put oil on the path at the exact place where the weakened branch was, where I slid into the water. I've pictures of all of this. You see, I remember that night. Jason insisted on going first, and he took my hand so that I would be right behind him. Just before I went down, he took one big step. He knew that oil was there. Why shouldn't he? He'd put it there!"

A commotion went through the courtroom. Jason buried his face in his hands. Kent Cooke leaned forward in his chair, nodding slowly at her revelations. The lawyer lost all pretense of friendliness.

"I'll remind you, young lady, this is not a stage where your dramatics are appreciated. For you to state, based on the evidence you have presented, that Jason purposely arranged for you to drown is absurd. Especially in light of how he risked his own life to save yours. Now—"

"He didn't want me to drown," she interrupted. "He wasn't going to weep if I did, but it's obvious that he wanted to rescue me."

The lawyer laughed at her. "You are confused, girl. Why would he do all these contradictory things? What was his motive?"

This lawyer was a fool. He'd asked a question he didn't realize she had the answer to. "To look like a hero," she said bitterly. "To get rid of the cowardly image he deserves. He is a coward, and a violent jerk. He almost took my head off that same night 'cause I wouldn't put out for him. I guess Karen wouldn't put out for him, either!"

The lawyer spoke to the judge. "Your honor, I ask

that this young lady's testimony be stricken from the record. It contains numerous self-contradictory statements."

"Overruled." The judge looked down at her. "Miss Jones, would it be possible for you to return tomorrow at this same time? I would like to give the district attorney an opportunity to cross-examine you, and to see your pictures."

She nodded. "I'll be here, your honor."

The judge called for an overnight recess. The district attorney asked for her phone number as she was leaving the room, saying he would be talking to her that evening. Kent Cooke stopped her in the hallway.

"You weren't exaggerating when you told me this morning you had things to do," he said. "You've given me a lot of material for my next column."

"I'm glad," she said flatly.

Her tone caught him offguard. But then he nodded his head sympathetically. "That was pretty stupid what I just said. I'm sorry." He squeezed her arm. "Please give my condolences to Ray's family."

"I will."

When he had gone, she looked around for the exit, anxious to get back on the road. Jason caught her before she could get to the door. There were tears in his eyes.

The poor baby bastard.

"Cindy, why are you doing this to me?" he cried.

"I swore to tell the truth, the whole truth, and nothing but the truth. Now get out of my way. I get nauseated around scum like you."

"Wait!" he pleaded, grabbing her arm.

"Don't touch me," she said, her breath cold.

He let her go, backed up a step. "Give me five minutes, Cindy. You owe me that much."

"All I owe you is a good spit in the face."

"Two minutes. Just let me explain. Please?"

She put on an expression of infinite boredom. "Start your lies."

Jason glanced around nervously. "Not out here in the open." He pointed to an empty room across the hall. "Let's go in there."

"No way I'm going in there alone with you."

"For god's sakes, Cindy, I'll leave the door open."

"All the way open," she said, agreeing reluctantly.

Once in the room Jason put on the same phony tone as his lawyer. "I honestly care about you. I would never do anything to harm you. When you fell in the river, I did everything I could to get you out."

"You did everything you could to put me in the river! Now you admit that right now or I'm leaving this instant! Right after I kick you in the balls!"

"Is this off the record?"

"I'll decide that. Speak."

Jason humbled his stance. "All right, all right, I did set it up so you would slip. But you were never in danger. I checked out the movements of the current thoroughly that afternoon. I threw in tiny Styrofoam balls and watched where they went. I knew if you were still in the water when you reached the overhanging tree, you'd pass directly beneath where I'd be waiting."

"Tiny Styrofoam balls?" She punched him in the chest. "I am a human being! I would have died if I'd gone over those falls!"

"I would have caught you first, Cindy."

"You don't know that! Your grip could have slipped!"

Jason shook his head, looked pained. "I didn't intend for anyone to get hurt."

"I don't believe that. What if more than one of us had gone in the water? What would you have done then? Choose who to save? What if my brother had slipped?"

"That could never have happened. As soon as you went in, I knew everybody would turn and go after you."

Cindy nodded grimly. "You had it all figured out. Well, you should've spent more time cleaning up your oil. Now you'll have to excuse me. I have to go home and cry about what you did to Ray."

Jason appeared puzzled. "Ray? What's wrong with Ray?"

She glared. "I hope you go straight to hell after you're executed."

Jason grabbed her again as she tried to get away. "What's wrong with Ray?" he demanded.

"The same thing that's wrong with Karen!" she yelled, slapping away his hands. "He's dead!"

"That's impossible. When did he die?"

"You should know!"

"But I didn't kill Ray. I didn't kill Karen! Cindy, you don't think I'm capable of murder?"

"Capable? I think you enjoy it."

"I didn't kill anybody! Listen to me!"

"No! You're sick!"

He stared at her for a moment, appalled at the hate he was seeing, and then the last visage of strength seemed to go out of him. "I'm not sick," he moaned, turning away and burying his face in the wall. "I was just scared."

Cindy was curious in spite of herself. There had been an uncanny ring of truth in his last words. "What were you scared of?"

He was weeping. He wouldn't look at her. "We were hanging out by the waterfall. We'd brought a blanket. Karen had brought it. I thought she was trying to tell me something. I knew she wasn't a virgin. I'd heard the stories about her and Ray. I figured we'd make it. We had fooled around enough. We were fooling around that night. But Karen got mad at me. She had a temper. She hit me in the face, scratched me with her nails. I chewed her out, told her she could walk home, and stalked off."

"This is B.S." But this did explain where the flesh under Karen's nails, that the coroner had uncovered, had come from.

Jason took his head off the wall, rubbing his red eyes. "No, this is the truth. And I wouldn't have really left her. I planned on heading back to the car and waiting for her to show."

"And she never showed?"

His lips trembled. "I'd just left her. I was on the other side of that granite mound I'd told the police about. I heard Karen say something. It sounded like she was talking to someone. I didn't know what was going on. There was no one else up there. Then I heard—I heard this shriek. It was awful."

"Karen?"

"It wasn't Karen. It was some kind of animal. I'd never heard anything like it before. Then Karen was shouting for me. She was screaming my name over and over again. But I couldn't go to her."

"Why not?"

He was having difficulty breathing. "I told you, I was scared. The shriek was getting louder. It was like a high, shrill strangling sound. There's no way to describe it. When I'm in bed at night, I still hear it. And I have these horrible dreams."

"Go on."

"I ran. I didn't know what else to do. I couldn't help Karen. I could hear the thing tearing her apart. Then Karen stopped screaming my name, and I knew she was dead. I ran all the way to the car."

"And the bump on your head?"

"I did that to myself."

"Why?"

"Can't you see why? I'd acted like a coward. No one would be able to understand why. No one would believe me if I told them what I'd heard. I had to make up an excuse."

"There was no bear?"

"I didn't see one."

Cindy considered. "Your excuse didn't fool many people."

"Because that damn thing didn't leave Karen where it had killed her! How was I supposed to know it would throw her in the river?"

"That *thing?* What was that thing?"

Jason shivered. "I don't know."

"How convenient."

His eyes were pleading. "You believe me, don't you, Cindy?"

"I believe in an awful monster. But you're him. You're a sick dude. You need to be locked up. I'm going to make sure you are."

"But I'm telling you the truth!"

"If what you said is true, you'd never have gone within a hundred miles of Crystal Falls again. But you dragged us all up there in the dark."

"I knew the thing must be gone. The entire area had been searched by the police. I felt safe going back up there with all my friends."

"And I felt safe being with my boyfriend," she muttered sarcastically.

A police officer, who'd been in the courtroom, was calling for her out in the hallway. Leaving Jason in his self-inflicted anguish, she hurried to find out what the gentleman wanted.

"There's a call for you, Miss Jones. It's a Pam Alta. She says it's urgent."

"Pam? Where can I take it?"

"This way."

The policeman led her to an office where a number of secretaries were typing furiously. She had to cup the phone to her ear to hear. "Pam?"

"Cindy, thank God I found you. I've been calling all over. Your mom told me you might still be at the hearing."

She could hear people being paged in the background. "Where are you, Pam?"

"At the hospital."

"Ray! Is he still alive?"

"No," Pam said weakly. "It's something else. It's Bala. He's been attacked, too. They're operating on him now. But before they wheeled him in, he told me I had to get ahold of you and Alex. He said your lives are in danger."

"In danger? How?"

"I don't know. He wouldn't talk to me. He seemed especially worried about your brother."

"But what attacked Bala?"

"It must have been some kind of animal. It messed him up pretty bad. Cindy, you have to come here. I can't handle all this by myself."

Some kind of animal.

Cindy closed her eyes. Was the whole world going nuts? There couldn't be a monster on the loose in Timber. The town was too straight to have one. "Have you been able to get hold of Alex?" she asked.

"No. I've tried everywhere. He's not at school. He's not at home. He's not at your parents' store."

"Keep trying. I'm on my way."

Cindy broke the connection and got hold of the

operator. She had her dial the Lee residence, charging the call to her home phone. It was Joni who answered.

"Hello?"

"Joni, this is Cindy. Have you seen my brother?"

"No."

"Have you talked to him today?"

"No."

"If he should stop by, could you have him call my parents' store or our house?"

"Yes."

"Good. Thank you."

"You're welcome."

Cindy put down the phone. That girl was weird. Alex should stay away from her.

"Who was that?" Alex asked.

"No one," Joni said, hanging up the phone, returning to her seat beside him at the kitchen table. Mrs. Lee had been right; Joni was looking wonderful. Her cheeks were flushed with life. She had on a beautiful white dress, and her shiny black hair hung over her shoulders with natural abandon. He was having a hard time taking his eyes off her.

From Pam's house, he'd driven straight to Joni's. He'd had to sit and listen to Mrs. Lee for almost two hours, all the time asking himself why he wasn't calling the police. In the end, what had probably kept him from such drastic action had been the rising conviction that he must have misunderstood Bala. The guy was as gentle as a butterfly. Why would he want to hurt Joni? And his patience had been rewarded when Joni had shown up safe and sound. Though Alex was still a bit confused as to what had gone on. Joni had returned, driving his car, without Bala.

Mrs. Lee was a case. The whole time he'd been waiting with her, she hadn't stopped talking about how worried she was. But then, ten minutes before Joni had returned home, she'd run off to do her shopping. Alex was beginning to think the aunt didn't really like Joni.

"Was it a wrong number?" he asked.

She nodded, regarding him curiously. "Why did you happen to come over just now, Alex?"

"I was concerned about you. Last week you didn't come to school. Then when I learned about what happened to Ray, I thought you'd be feeling bad."

She sipped her tea, which she'd prepared for both of them. She made it strong and drank it plain. "It was sad about Ray," she said.

"Does your aunt know what happened? I got the impression she just thought he'd disappeared."

Joni shook her head. "I never told her the details."

"I see. Well, do you know what happened?"

She continued to stare at him. "How should I know?"

"He dropped you off and you didn't see him again?"

"Yes."

"That's how I thought it probably went." He sat back in his chair. He couldn't quit thinking about the way Ray had died. Torn to pieces like Karen. He hoped to God it had been quick, that he hadn't suffered.

"What are you thinking?" Joni asked.

Alex played with his spoon and cup. "About Ray. He was my pal and I never—I never treated him with the same kindness he treated me." He sighed. "I still can't believe this has happened."

"He seemed like a nice boy."

"I'm glad you got a chance to know him a bit." Alex chuckled, a lump in his throat. "He was such a character."

"He was very attached to me."

"Yeah, he was. He had a crush on you. I didn't know you knew."

Joni's eyes watched him above the rim of her cup. "I can always tell."

"Can you?"

"Always."

Alex began to fidget, thinking he should leave, not sure why. "So you left my keys in the ignition?"

"Yes."

"Did you drop Bala off at home?"

"I dropped him off, yes." Joni put down her cup. "Alex, tell me why you are here."

"I told you."

"But Bala spoke to you. I know this. What did he say?"

"He said, ah—just a bunch of weird stuff."

"Tell me?"

"Why?"

Joni's eyes were more exotic and more fascinating than even he could remember, so black and deep with their hypnotic flecks of color; greens and purples floating around wide pupils. Her cold or flu or whatever had been bothering her must be completely gone. Except for maybe in her throat. She sounded more hoarse than usual. "Because I want to know," she said.

Alex laughed nervously. "He said I had to stay away from you. He was talking like a madman."

"Did he tell you why you should stay away?"

He picked up his spoon again. It felt strangely heavy. "I don't like talking about this. Bala's a great guy."

"Did he tell you I killed Ray?"

Alex shrugged, trying to keep his gaze down, not succeeding. "He implied it, yes. Like I said, he seemed to be very confused."

Joni closed her eyes for a moment, sitting so still she could have stopped breathing. Then she appeared to come to a decision. Standing suddenly, she began to clear away the dishes. "Alex, could you take me for a ride?"

"Sure. Where would you like to go?"

"Up to the waterfall, where we can be alone."

CHAPTER

XI

THE WAITING LOUNGE in Timber Memorial for the friends and relatives of those undergoing surgery was depressing. The decor was a harsh white and the few paintings cluttering the walls were so cheap and flat that it would have been better had no one bothered to hang them up. Of course, Cindy realized, you couldn't have posters of rock 'n' roll bands looking over your shoulder while you were waiting to hear if a loved one was going to live or die.

"So you didn't think the blow to his head was real serious?" Cindy asked Pam. She'd asked Pam the same question two hours before when she'd arrived at the hospital but she wanted further reassurance.

"He was conscious," Pam said, bags under her eyes. "Isn't that supposed to be a good sign?"

"They wouldn't have operated on his arm and his side if they were worried about brain damage," Mrs. Alta said. The short middle-aged lady sat across from them reading a *People* magazine. She had been studying the same page since Cindy had arrived.

"I wish Alex would call," Cindy said. And this, too, was something she'd said before. There was a west-facing window in the hallway outside the waiting room. The sun had recently set. Night was coming quickly.

154

"Did you leave a message at Ray's house?" Pam asked.

"Yes."

"Did you talk to his mother?" Mrs. Alta asked.

"No, his father. He could hardly speak. I felt bad for bothering them."

"I feel bad." Pam nodded vaguely. She wasn't totally with it yet. Cindy gave her a hug.

"Mrs. Alta?" a doctor said, appearing in the doorway of the lounge. Attired entirely in green, he must have come straight from the operating theater. "Bala's going to be all right. The operation went smoothly."

Pam's mother stood and squeezed her palms together. "Thank God."

"Can we see him?" Cindy asked, also standing.

"Not now, he's in the recovery room," the doctor said. "He should be there at least an hour; the operation was complicated. His left elbow was badly broken and we had to remove numerous bone splinters from his rib cage. He also has a concussion and has lost a lot of blood. But his vital signs are stable. The anesthesiologist said he's never seen an individual with such a hardy constitution." The surgeon glanced at the clock on the wall. "It's getting late. I would suggest all of you forget about seeing him this evening. When he gets back to his room, he'll be groggy. And, in either case, it will be better if he's allowed to rest."

"But I have to talk to him," Cindy insisted. "I can't wait until tomorrow. I can't wait an hour."

"Cindy," Mrs. Alta said, "let's do what the doctor says. Come home with us. You can stay for dinner. This has been a long day for all of us. And maybe later tonight we could talk to Bala on the phone, if he's feeling up to it."

The doctor nodded. He had a worn, hardened look

and didn't appear the type who could be talked into anything. "That sounds like the best course."

Cindy took a step toward the surgeon. "You don't understand, Doctor. Before he was taken into the operating room, Bala said he had something very important to tell me. I must insist I be allowed to see him right now."

The doctor crossed his arms across his chest, assuming a slightly amused expression. "You must insist? I'm afraid, young lady, the policy of this hospital cannot be bent to conform to your wishes."

"But—" Cindy began.

"But if you won't be able to sleep tonight without seeing him," the doctor interrupted, "you can wait until he is returned to his room. I will leave word with the nurse that you may have a few minutes with him. Please do not abuse this favor."

"But—" Cindy said.

The doctor raised his hand. "Don't argue with me." He looked at Mrs. Alta. "I have to go now, but I'll be in tomorrow afternoon. Call and make an appointment with my secretary. The name is Dr. Wheeler. We'll need to discuss the details of Bala's rehabilitation."

"Thank you, Doctor," Mrs. Alta said. The man nodded and walked away. "He seems a competent gentleman," Mrs. Alta remarked.

"He reminds me of that joke," Cindy muttered. "The one with the punch line, 'Oh, that's God, he thinks he's a doctor.'"

Naturally Mrs. Alta tried to talk her out of staying. But not knowing why Bala was desperate to speak with her, why he was specifically worried about Alex, Cindy felt she had no choice but to wait. Pam offered to keep her company, but Mrs. Alta said no, and so

Cindy was left alone to watch the clock and the darkness outside, getting deeper and deeper.

When the better part of an hour had gone by, a nurse finally came for her and led her to a room on the second floor, instructing her not to tire Bala. Cindy promised she would not overstay her welcome.

The room contained a large window, which looked south in the direction of Castle Park. The shadows of the mountains were clearly visible, cutting a jagged black line across the almost black sky. Inside, the only illumination was a red night light above the sink. Bala had the room to himself, his covered feet poking over the end of the bed, his face almost buried beneath a wad of bandages. He stirred as she entered and she quickly moved to his side. His left arm and shoulder were encased in a cast. Dried blood caked his lips. His open eyelids looked heavy.

"How do you feel?" she asked, taking his right hand.

He swallowed painfully, whispered, "I will live. Where is Alex?"

"I don't know," she said, the panic coming hard and fast. "We can't find him. What does Alex have to do with what happened to you?"

"Why can you not locate him?"

"I don't know," she repeated. "I thought you could tell me."

"Have you tried Joni's house?"

"Yes. I left a message there that if he comes by, he's to immediately call my parents. They know where I am."

"Who did you leave the message with?"

"Joni."

Bala winced. "Call again, now. See if the aunt is there. Find out what you can."

Cindy didn't question his order. There was a phone

around the corner and change in her pocket. Information gave her the number—she'd forgotten it—and Joni's aunt answered on the second ring.

"Hello?"

"Mrs. Lee, this is Cindy Jones. I'm Alex's sister. Is he there by any chance?"

"No. He was here earlier, but he left."

"Did he leave with Joni?"

"I don't know. I had to go out for groceries."

"Was Joni there before you left?"

"No. I don't know if she's been home all day. If he comes by, should I have him call you?"

"I'd appreciate that. I'm at Timber Memorial. He can have me paged. Please have him, or Joni, call me the second they get there. This is very important."

"What are you doing at the hospital, dear?"

"A friend of mine has been hurt. I have to go now, Mrs. Lee."

Bala took the information hard. The flesh beneath the bandage that circled the top of his head paled, if that was possible. "Pray he did not leave with her," he whispered.

"What's the matter?" she cried, unable to bear the tension. "How can Joni harm him?"

Bala glanced at the cast binding his left arm. "It was she who did this to me."

"But that's impossible. She's just a girl!"

Bala rolled his eyes toward her. What she saw in those eyes, or didn't see, frightened her even more than his next words. There was no hope there. It was as though he had already buried her brother in his thoughts. "She is not a girl, Cindy. She is not a human being. She is something else, something horrible."

Alex was glad the moon was full. Few people who lived in the city could appreciate how bright the moon was when it didn't have to compete with kilowatts of artificial light, how safe and comfortable it was to hike beneath its silvery orb. Joni couldn't have picked a better night for an impulsive stroll in the woods.

They were standing next to the top of the waterfall, on the exact spot where Wolf had tried to shove Jason over the edge. A stiff breeze was dragging up through the gorge, creating a dull echoing roar, which seemed to throb with a living beat, lifting a faint spray from the tumbling river and sprinkling it round their heads. Alex pulled Joni close, trying to keep her warm, hoping she would lean over and kiss the side of his face.

"Do you want to head back?" he asked after a long spell of silence between them.

"No," she said quietly, staring into the distance. "I want to fly. I want to fly away."

Alex glanced down, shuddering slightly. They were *very* close to the brink, much closer than he would have chosen to come himself. Heights seemed to have no effect on Joni. "That would be a handy talent to have on this ledge," he agreed.

She turned toward him, her face only inches away. That was a wondrous thing about her; no matter which way she turned, the moon always seemed to be in her eyes. "You're afraid of falling?"

"Well, I'm not really afraid." He laughed. "But I'd rather not fall, if that's what you mean."

"That's what I mean," she said.

"What?"

She swept her hand up his back, into his hair, tugging at the strands with a force that was close to painful. "I remember the first time I came up here. I felt at home, even though there was all this water. I'd never seen water flowing like this before, but it didn't scare me."

"Doesn't it rain a lot in England?"

"I suppose."

He frowned. "Don't you know?"

"I know more of a place I haven't told you of."

He would sort that one out later. "Did you come up here before I took you?"

"Yes. But I also remember that night with you. It was special for me. It was something a young girl would do, something she would enjoy. I was pleased I could enjoy it with you."

Alex cleared his throat, not sure if he was hearing her properly with the rushing water and the moaning wind, "I'm glad you had a nice time. But are you sure you don't want to start back? It's getting late."

Her stroking of his hair softened and deepened, so that she was now massaging his scalp. Alex had the amusing thought that this was something he often did to Wolf. He wasn't complaining. The sensation was relaxing; he was actually beginning to feel slightly drowsy. Everything that had happened during the day seemed nothing more than a collection of dream images that he would be able to awake from soon.

"We're not going back," Joni said.

"We have to. We can't spend the night up here."

Joni appeared to agree with him, contradicting her previous statement in the process. "I wish this night didn't have to be so short."

Alex swayed slightly on his feet. This was no place to forget where his shoes were planted. He took a step backward, pulling Joni with him. She lost her hold on his head. "We could do something else," he said. I'm not big on junk food, but there's a coffee shop in town that serves the greatest doughnuts. Are you hungry?"

She glanced behind her at the edge, then stared at him, the cold light of the moon making her face appear deathly pale. The wind had taken ahold of her thick hair, and it flapped on the right side of her head like a single huge black wing. "Alex, I'm always hungry."

Bala had requested a glass of water. Cindy brought him a small cup from the hospital room sink, supporting the back of his head while he sipped it. His last statement had driven away all her questions. She no longer knew what to ask. She would have to listen first, for a bit, and see whether Bala was crazy, or if the world was. Pulling up a seat, she settled beside his bed.

"You were right," he began, his voice smoother with the gulp of water. "The boy I spoke of in psychology class was myself. Like my father, I was learning to be a shaman. Starting at such an early age, I was about eight at the time, is unusual. Traditionally, an individual has to wait until he has entered puberty. But my grandfather saw great potential in me. Many times he told me that one day I would be a powerful Bairavee.

"There were a number of things he taught me. I will not go into them all. It is only the ancient technique of transferring a human's soul into an animal's body that need concern us now. In this area my grandfather gave me a lot of experience. You must understand it was always he who took care of the details of the transfer. To this day, I do not know half of what he would do."

Bala closed his eyes. "I remember those days as though they were a part of last week. I remember the sound of my grandfather's voice as I sank deeper and deeper into myself. Stillness is a prerequisite for undergoing any shamic journey. The uniqueness of the silence he could induce was that I could experience it with my eyes open. Unless your sight is in use, no transfer is possible. This is true for the animal participant as well as for the human. You must be staring at each other.

"As I said in class, all types of animals were used. Once I was even sent into a snake. That was a strange day. I remember the feel of the dust on my scaly hide as I slithered over the ground. Yet that was only a small part of the phenomenon. I *was* a snake. I had snake thoughts and feelings. Do not ask me to explain what they were like. It was beautiful and it was horrible. You would need to know the reptile's language to even get the faintest idea of what I went through. And, yes, snakes have a language. My grandfather says every creature on earth does.

"These 'trips' all took place over a period of six months. At the end of that time, my father died and I lost interest. There, I am putting it mildly. Actually, I became furious with my grandfather. I would not speak to him. But it may not have been entirely his fault. My father had tried to use an esoteric skill he had still to master. That was one of my father's weaknesses, and the reason my grandfather knew he would never be a true Bairavee. My father had no patience. He tried to dominate a spirit in the netherworld, and the spirit killed him. At least this was what my grandfather told me. Not that the details meant much to me then. My father was gone and my mother was a widow. I could see little benefit to be had from becoming a shaman, and much harm, and I wanted nothing to do with it. This upset my grandfather a great deal.

"The years went by and the famine started and it was hard just to stay alive. I had no time to worry about magic and whether I was depriving myself of important experiences. Then Dr. Herbert Stevens and his wife, Valerie, came to live in our village. I mentioned them in Miss Clemens's class. The doctor was a very busy man. I did not have a lot of contact with him. But his wife took a special liking to me. I liked her, too; she was a great woman. She taught me how to read and speak English. She had boxes of books imported from London, where the Stevens were originally from. I learned a lot from those books. I discovered that most of the suffering we were going through was our own fault. This was probably unfair, but I totally blamed our tradition of Bairavees for keeping us so backward. As a result, the distance between my grandfather and me became greater.

"One hot and hungry day, it was about a year ago, another doctor and his wife visited our village. They were friends of the Stevenses. They had come to Mau Dogan for the same reason, to help us, but planned on staying only a month. They had a beautiful sixteen-year-old daughter."

"Joni Harper?" Cindy whispered.

Bala opened his eyes and looked at her. "Yes, it was Joni. She was not like you know her now. She was vibrant, full of life. She was also headstrong, maybe even snobbish, but I found her quite charming. Oh, I did not tell you this. Despite my grandfather's disdain for the 'outside' world, he could speak English. This should not surprise you. He has perfect recall. Joni was always talking to him, always after him to show her magic, which would amuse my grandfather. Yet he gave her much of his time, and at first this did not make sense to me. But I was to learn the reason soon enough.

"Joni was a find for him. There were others in my village who had the potential to experience trance states. The ability is not that rare, not as rare as the potential to become a full-fledged shaman, which is quite another matter. Joni had the ability. And she had something else my grandfather thought could be used. She was not a product of our traditions. She was a skeptic. He knew I saw her that way. His plan was to prove to her that his powers were real. You see, by this time—this was years after my adventures in other bodies—I had come to the conclusion that the shamic experience was nothing but an illusion. My grandfather wanted to use Joni to respark my interest."

Bala paused. "It was a terrible mistake on his part to try these things on an outsider."

"Did Joni go into an animal?" Cindy asked.

Bala took a breath. "Yes."

Outside the window the silhouettes of the mountain peaks appeared to glow; the moon was rising swiftly. Cindy wasn't sure, but it seemed she could see Crystal Falls, sparkling faintly like a net of fine wires exposed to a shorting circuit. Had Joni taken her brother to that lonely spot, where Karen and Ray had died? She swallowed. "What was the animal?"

Bala's cheek twitched. "A vulture."

Cindy jerked as if she had been struck. "What happened?"

Bala sighed. "I saw the whole thing. I tried to stop it. But my grandfather is not one to argue with, and he had Joni on his side. She had not the slightest fear. Her parents were away visiting a nearby village. She wanted to do it before they came back.

"My grandfather lured a vulture out of the air. This was not a major feat for him; there were plenty of vultures about in those days, always waiting for another one of us to die. He tied the bird in front of the girl, sang his trance-inducing chants. Both Joni and the vulture went very still, staring into each other's eyes. Initially, all appeared to be going well. Then the bird began to thrash violently, shrieking with a noise that would chill your heart if you had heard it. Joni was inside, and she was terrified.

"What it was like for that poor girl, we can only imagine. During all the experiments I performed as a child, I had never gone into a vulture. You could not have forced me into one; they are disgusting creatures, always hovering about, wanting you to die, wishing they had the strength and courage to kill you. I do not know why my grandfather did not chose another creature. But that was not his only mistake that day.

"Joni's fear was not totally unexpected. Quickly my grandfather moved to reverse the transfer. Unfortunately, the vulture had been bound at the foot with a simple string. In its fear, it bit through the string. My grandfather was able to grab it, for a moment, but it twisted free and flew away. Or I should say, Joni flew away."

Cindy trembled. "She was still inside?"

"Had you asked me at the time, I probably would have told you she was not. I still did not believe in soul transfer. But after what has happened in Timber in the last few days, I do not know. That vulture took off and headed directly to the next village, where Joni's parents were having lunch outside. It went straight to their table. Scared them badly, from what I was later told. The father reached for his rifle. He blew the bird's head off."

"He killed his own daughter?" Cindy asked, horrified.

"Perhaps. He killed the vulture she had supposedly gone into. There was a piece of string still tied around its leg."

"And how was Joni?"

Bala coughed painfully. "My grandfather said Joni was dead."

"You mean, her body died?"

"No," he said, wheezing. "Her body was still alive, though she was almost comatose. Valerie was there. She had seen the whole thing, too. She did not believe in my grandfather's powers, but she did not disbelieve in them, either. She knew something traumatic had happened to the girl, and she heeded my grandfather's command that no one be allowed near Joni, even her own parents. Do not ask me how he knew the vulture had been slain before the rest of us. There simply was something in Joni's eyes that told him there was no going back.

"When the parents returned to Mau Dogan that evening, they told everyone about the vulture attack at their lunch table. The news set off a stir, though the Harpers did not know the reasons behind it. Naturally, they wondered where Joni was. My grandfather wanted to stall them. He had Valerie tell them Joni had gone for an overnight hike with some of the village girls. The Harpers thought that was nice. They were not concerned.

"Joni seemed to be in shock. Along with Valerie and my grandfather, I stayed with her throughout the night. She kept looking about, turning her neck in strange ways, and making funny sounds in her throat. Not once did she show signs of violence. But her eyes had a peculiar glint in them. I felt uncomfortable when she looked at me. It was as if she was wondering if she could eat me.

"But I still honestly believed her problems were psychological in nature, brought on by her terrifying experience. I had read several books by English psychiatrists, and considered myself something of an expert on the mind—what conceit. I wanted her turned over to her parents, who could get her professional help. My grandfather dismissed the idea. He said we must not let the vulture out of our sight. Already, he had done away with Joni's name.

"Valerie did not know what to do. Her husband was away for a week, in a village two hundred miles to the south. For the most part, she agreed with me. Except when Joni looked right at her. Then she had her doubts.

"The Harpers did not stay long satisfied with the excuses they were fed to explain Joni's absence. They began to get suspicious. The following night my grandfather had Joni transferred to a village much smaller than Mau Dogan. It was located in some nearby hills. Valerie went with her. She was afraid to do so, but I think she felt a responsibility to look after the girl since it was obvious my grandfather was not going to relinquish her voluntarily. Oh, this is an important point. Valerie had known Joni since she was young, and had always loved her.

"I did not go. I never saw Valerie again."

Cindy's trembling refused to stop. She wished *he* would stop. But she had to know. "What happened?"

"The Harpers started to get angry. They became convinced that we had kidnapped Joni. They started to make threats. My grandfather finally told them the truth. Of course, they thought he was mad. When they saw they were not going to get past my grandfather, they went running to the authorities. In my country that is not an easy thing to do. The system moves slowly. It was several days before they returned with help. By then we had heard word that Valerie was dead and that Joni was beginning to talk again. Also, during this time, Dr. Herbert Stevens came back from his trip. It was awful telling him about his wife. They had been together many years."

"How did Valerie die?" Cindy asked.

"The same way as Karen and Ray."

Cindy nodded weakly, her eyes beginning to burn. "Go on."

"My grandfather was more anxious than ever about Joni. Hours before the government people arrived, he dragged me to the place we had hidden her. The change in her was dramatic. She seemed much more *human*. She could even identify certain things by name. Although upset about Valerie—I did not yet know, or did not believe, it had been Joni who had killed her—I was relieved. Joni appeared to be improving. But my grandfather reacted differently. He said we had to kill the girl immediately."

Bala stopped, staring off into space for over a minute. Cindy finally asked, "Do you need to rest?"

He blinked, and resumed speaking in a softer voice. "I was thinking about what my grandfather told me then. Remember, although I was trying to be a logical scientific young man, I had been conditioned to the bizarre all my life. Yet what he said as we stood outside Joni's hut went beyond anything I had ever heard. Joni had killed Valerie, he said, and she had done so in order to steal the life from her *sheath*. I am using the closest English word I can find. The actual term he used was *manas*. You almost have to be a shaman to understand what your manas is. It is not an individual's spirit, nor is it the body; it is, rather, the immaterial substance that keeps the two wedded together. By killing Valerie, Joni had been able to *feed* on Valerie's humanity via her sheath. Do you understand?"

"No."

"We are more than animals. Your Western religions say we have a soul. A Bairavee would agree with that. But a Bairavee would add that we have a sheath that provides a connection between the physical world and the spiritual world. Apparently, when the spirit of the vulture got trapped in Joni's body, it inherited her brain and all the knowledge that was stored inside. But it could not use the knowledge. It lacked the connector. It lacked the sheath."

"Are you saying the vulture wanted to be human?"

"That's a penetrating question. Certainly, it could not be a bird anymore. But maybe it was the other way around. Maybe what was left of the real Joni wanted to be human again. Who knows? It could be that my grandfather created something that was neither animal nor human, but something different, something wholly unnatural. All I knew for sure at the time was that my grandfather insisted it must be destroyed before it destroyed others.

"But I was not going to let him kill her. I was still hoping she could be cured. Ignoring my grandfather's pleas, I picked her up and literally carried her all the way back to Mau Dogan, to her parents and the angry officials. And then she was gone, and we did not hear anything about her for a while. Dr. Herbert Stevens left the area shortly afterward.

"Joni had a younger brother. He was in England when the Harpers had first visited, but Joni had often spoken of him. His name was Jim. It must have been six months after Joni had been carried off by her parents that I met Jim. I was sitting outside my mother's hut, when he suddenly appeared and demanded to know what had happened to his sister. He was extremely upset. It seemed Joni had torn his mother apart."

Cindy jumped to her feet, unable to contain the pressure building inside. "I can't listen to this. I have to go."

Bala tried to sit up. "Where are you going?"

"I have to see about Alex." She hurried toward the door. "I have to know where he is."

169

"Come back!" Bala called. "There is much more."

She ignored him, for the moment, hurrying to the phone she had used earlier. She was wasting her time. There was no answer at her own house; her parents said he hadn't been by the store; and Joni's aunt had nothing new to report. Cindy trudged back to Bala's room, collapsing in her chair. "Go on," she said wearily.

"Alex has not come in?"

She shook her head. "What happened next?"

Bala settled back into the pillow. "Jim had not come to our village by himself. His father had also returned, and was meeting with my grandfather to see if anything could be done for his daughter. Mr. Harper was a changed man. He was scared. He was ready to listen. But my grandfather gave him not a shred of hope. He repeated what he had said originally; the girl had to be killed. The son heard this, and he was convinced my grandfather was right. Jim was spooked. But the father would not hear of it."

"Where was Joni at this time?"

"It was my understanding she was in a mental hospital in England undergoing observation. The doctors could not find a whole lot wrong with her, except that she was unusually withdrawn. I guess absorbing the mother's sheath had improved Joni even more."

"But didn't the doctors know this girl was a murderer?"

"No, they did not. Harper was not even sure Joni had killed his wife, though Jim swore she had. You can see why Mr. Harper had trouble believing his own son. Joni simply would not have had the strength to do what had been done to Mrs. Harper. Scotland Yard was out looking for an animal."

"How is it Joni didn't kill any of the doctors in the hospital?"

"Because Joni does not kill strangers. She only kills those who love her."

"What?"

"My grandfather says the emotional attachment is necessary for her to be able to absorb an individual's sheath."

"But her own mother—What if she loves someone in return?"

"If she is this soulless human, would she love anyone?"

"But Alex is completely attached to her!"

Bala sighed. "I know. I told him to stay away from her."

Cindy fought to calm herself. The more information she could get, the better chance she would have of saving Alex. Not for a moment did she disbelieve Bala's story. All the bizarre killings lately made it impossible to doubt him. "What happened next?"

"Mr. Harper and his son left. This time my grandfather did not let the issue rest. Although he lives in a poor village in the middle of nowhere, he is fairly well known and respected in my country. There are even people in the government who have come to him for spiritual help. He went to such an official now, someone who owed him a favor, and said he wanted his grandson—me—sent to England to keep an eye on Joni. The official agreed; he was confident he could use the student exchange program to get me to London. But then this official learned Joni was being sent to America, to a city called Timber."

"But what happened to Mr. Harper and his son?"

"Mr. Harper was found ripped to pieces. This time the police suspected the son. He seemed crazy. He kept telling everyone that his beautiful sister was really a vulture. Jim Harper's now in a mental institution."

A disturbing realization hit her, and with it came anger. "But none of this makes sense. You knew Joni's history when you arrived here. You were nice to her. You treated her like she was a human being!"

"I thought she was."

"After all you'd seen and heard? I find that hard to believe."

"When I left Mau Dogan and came to this country, it was like a dream come true. I felt I had entered the real world and left the superstitions of my youth behind. When I rode in your beautiful cars past your tall glass buildings, I could hardly remember, much less believe, my grandfather's warnings."

"Are you serious? What of Valerie and Mr. and Mrs. Harper? These people were butchered. Surely you didn't think that was all due to bad luck on their part?"

Bala sounded defensive. "When I got here, the first thing I did was go to see Joni. Had she scared me the way she had that night after the accident, I might have done something. But she did not frighten me at all. She was not glad to see me—she knew who I was— but she was not rude. She seemed your typical teenage girl."

"That chick never seemed typical to me," Cindy said bitterly.

"But you encouraged your brother to go out with her?"

"I didn't know she had people for lunch!"

"I did not know that, either. When I looked at her, I could not imagine her killing anyone. Understand, everything I had heard about her violence had been secondhand. Also, you must remember, I still did not believe my grandfather's talents were genuine."

"But what about what happened to Karen? Didn't her death convince you?"

"I never heard about Karen until that day I asked you about her."

"It wasn't Karen who reintroduced you to Joni?" Pam had said that had been the case, although she'd been unsure. When Cindy thought about it, she figured Karen must have been dead at least three weeks before Bala arrived in Timber.

"No."

"Why did you bring up these spirit-swapping experiments in Miss Clemens's class if you thought they were all bunk?"

"You prodded me into discussing them."

"I think you had another reason. You were wanting to see if Joni would react."

"The idea did cross my mind," Bala admitted. "But I do not even think she was listening when I was talking."

Cindy shook her head in disgust. "You still should have warned Alex."

"How? I warned him today and he ignored me. He is infatuated with her. She could have drunk his blood, and he would have passed it off to bad upbringing. Until this morning, I was glad she was going out with Alex. I wanted her to have the chance to do the things normal girls do. She told me herself this is what she wanted."

"Why did your grandfather send you?" she asked. "Why didn't he come himself?"

"He is old, almost blind. He had faith in my abilities to deal with her."

"What abilities are these?"

"You spotted some of them. And you guessed how they came to me. Every time I went into an animal—I feel now this must have been the case—I took from it whatever special talents it possessed."

"So it was a fish who taught you how to swim?" she said sarcastically.

Bala stared at the ceiling. "You hate me. I suppose I cannot blame you. It was simply impossible for me to believe the impossible."

She went to snap at him again, stopped herself. He had his reasons for not warning them, but she believed he was omitting the most important one, although the lapse may have been unintentional. He had mentioned how he had been charmed by Joni. The truth of the matter, Cindy thought, was that he had loved her, as a sister perhaps, maybe as a good friend, but loved nonetheless. He had not warned them because he had refused to admit the truth to himself. She debated about confronting him with it, but quickly decided it didn't matter. "You became a believer today," she said instead. "What happened?"

"When I heard of Ray's death, I got a handgun and drove straight to Joni's house. I told her I wanted to go for a walk. I think she knew I intended to kill her. But she was not afraid. She has a cold confidence. She is aware of her strength and speed. She suggested we should go up to the falls, where we all went that night. This did not surprise me. Vultures are territorial. The national park has become her new hunting ground. The place could serve my needs just as well. I could kill her, I thought, and bury her, and, with a little luck, not be sent to prison.

"We parked in that place we had before, Lot H. We did not take the same path, though, but headed through the trees toward the river. She was a couple of strides ahead of me. I took out my pistol. I did not even have a chance to fire it."

"Why not?" Cindy asked.

"It was probably my own fault. I hesitated, for the same old reason. She was a beautiful young girl. I could not shoot her in the back. And then it was too late. She turned and stared at me. Her large black eyes seemed to fill the world. Having been shown the way to leave her body once, she apparently has not forgotten how to leave it again. This must be how she gets a grip on an individual's sheath; she lets a portion of herself wrap around the person. I could not move, for a split second, and then it did not matter. Her reflexes are incredible, at least the equal of her strength. She snapped my arms behind my back and, keeping them pinned with one hand, dragged me toward the edge of a cliff near the base of the waterfall. She threw me over the side without saying a word."

"Why didn't she ravage your body like she had the others?"

"I think she only does that when she is absorbing an individual's sheath. Obviously, she was able to affect mine, but since there was not a strong bond between us, she was not able to use it. You could say I was a meal she could not digest."

"I wonder," Cindy said doubtfully, thinking again of his initial affection for Joni. Bala seemed to read her mind, and quickly offered another explanation.

"She has inherited Joni's brain. She has not assimilated everything Joni knew, but she is not stupid. She probably did not want to add to the mystery that is developing. She probably wanted it to look like I had accidentally fallen over the side. If the two men fishing around the bend in the river had not been there and pulled me out, I would have drowned. Her plan was shrewd."

"So she thinks you're dead?"

"I would assume. But that is not necessarily a good thing. I told Alex that Joni was dangerous. If he is

175

with her and spills that, she may feel she has to destroy him to keep the truth from spreading. Plus Joni might kill him for another reason."

"What? She can't want to suck on his sheath. She just had Ray's."

"But Alex is far more attached to her than Ray was. She stands to gain more from him than anybody since her own father."

"But you just said she doesn't want any more beat-up bodies lying around?"

Bala nodded. "I hope that factor outweighs her hunger."

Cindy stood and went to the sink, splashing cold water in her face, noting that her eyes were puffy. She must have been crying while listening to Bala; she hadn't realized it.

I can cry later. If Alex is dead, I'll have the rest of my life to cry.

"What if we call the police?" she said.

"They will not believe us."

"But this reporter told me the coroner refused to release the results of the autopsy on Karen. The coroner would only have done that if he couldn't figure out what they were dealing with. Somebody already knows something weird is going on."

"There is not a chance, nor will there ever be, that the police will believe that a cute English girl has the strength of a grizzly. I am surprised you believe me."

"I was a born believer," she muttered. "Why *is* she so strong? And why does she behave like a predator and not a scavenger? Vultures don't go after the living."

"Vultures are usually a bag of bones and feathers. But they can pull a surprising amount of weight into the air. They are very strong for their size."

"And now we have a ninety-nine-pound vulture?"

"Yes, you see my point. And in a sense, I have already answered your second question. Joni hungers to be human. She needs to feed on human sheaths to stay human. She does not actually eat the flesh. The effect of each of her feedings must eventually wear off, forcing her to kill again."

"Then she won't need to kill Alex," she blurted out, knowing she was repeating herself.

Bala was grim. "There is the other consideration. You ask why she behaves like a predator? I will tell you something your encyclopedias might not agree with. Vultures are predators at heart. They would kill any living creature if they could, if they had the strength Joni has, and not only for food. They are hideous beasts."

"You're not giving me much hope."

Bala's face was sad. "Maybe it is better this way, Cindy."

She exploded. "Damn you! I have hope! I'm not writing my brother off just like that!" She stepped toward his bed, glared down at him. "He's going to make it. He's smart and he's fast and he's not going to die! He might not even be with her!"

"I pray that he is not."

"I don't want your prayers! You're a shaman's grandson! I want magic! I want to know how I can waste this bitch!"

Bala was concerned. "I did not tell you this story so you would go after Joni."

"Then why did you tell me? So I would know not to invite her to my next slumber party?"

"I've been trying to warn you away from her. You are going to have to be patient. She has no idea I am here. Wait till I recover. Leave her to me."

Cindy stopped. "But she *will* know you're here. I told her aunt I was at the hospital, waiting to see a friend of mine who'd been hurt. She'll figure out who that friend is."

Bala frowned. "She could come here."

"I think she'll call first to speak to me, and see if I know anything. She wouldn't want to knock you off and not know if we'd talked about her past."

Bala nodded. "That is logical."

Cindy's voice shook. "It's also logical that if she has been with my brother, and calls instead of him . . ." She couldn't say it. She turned for the door. "I'm going up there."

"Where?"

"To her hunting ground, where else?"

Bala tried to sit up again. "Do not be foolish. That national park must cover thirty square miles. It is already dark. Where would you look? And even if by chance you did get close to her, she would see you before you saw her. And she would kill you, make no mistake about it."

She paused at the door. "I'll get someone to go with me."

"You are not going to convince anyone to help you search for a monster. Please, listen to me. Do not throw your life away. All we can do is wait for one of them to show up."

"All right," Cindy whispered, knowing he spoke the truth, looking out the window at the mountains. "But if she hurts Alex, that girl's going to wish she had stayed a bird. I'll kill her, I swear it."

They didn't go for doughnuts. Try as he might, Alex couldn't convince Joni they should start down the mountain. He was beginning to suspect she wanted to stay out past the time her aunt went to bed. She was stalling, that was for sure.

But he didn't let her have it all her own way. If they

were going to stay outside, he told her, they were going to stay warm. He was going to build a fire. He had a Bic lighter in his pocket, and there were plenty of dry sticks to be found nearby. To his surprise, Joni was against the idea. It seemed she was afraid of fires. And she had always struck him as the fearless type. But he insisted, and once he had a small blaze going beneath the overhanging ledge Bala had jumped from while rescuing his sister, Joni finally began to relax, and curled up beside him and the flames.

The wall of stone at their back provided a shield against the wind, and the icy splashings of the nearby river couldn't touch them. Collecting the wood for the fire had been invigorating, but now Alex began to feel drowsy again. The warmth from the flames was sinking softly into his bones, and even Joni's throaty voice was beginning to sound soothing. She was talking about her childhood. He was only half listening, and he assumed that was the reason half of what she said made no sense. One moment she was reminiscing about playing in green meadows, and the next, about drifting over wide desert stretches.

"Now just a minute," he interrupted, though it was really a big bother to do so. "You're saying you didn't live all your life in England?"

"I've lived two lives," she answered, sitting on her knees before his outstretched legs, her dangling hair a dark shade of red in the fiery light. "It's difficult for me to put them together. But I wanted you to hear of both of them so you would know why we're here. I want you to understand me."

"I'd like to," he said, yawning, wondering if she were referring to her life before her parents died, and her life after. Another thing continued to puzzle him; that remark her aunt had made about Joni's previous contact with Bala's people. All the while he had been waiting with Mrs. Lee for Joni to come home, the woman had tactfully avoided explaining what she'd meant. "Have you ever been to Africa?" he asked suddenly.

"Places don't say where I have been. Or where I have to go."

"But have you ever visited there? Bala's always treated you like he knew you from before."

She nodded carefully. "His is the first face I ever saw, after I found my way back."

"What do you mean?"

She leaned closer, her hair lying across him. Despite the mountain chill, she seemed perfectly comfortable in her simple white dress. "Let's not talk about him."

She had reacted the same way on his living room couch. "But is he an old friend?" he asked.

She smiled. "He's nothing now. He's gone."

"Gone? Where did he go?"

"Far away, where he won't have to worry about me anymore." She placed her hand on his shoulder, pulled him slowly toward her. "Are you worried about me, Alex?"

He grinned. "Should I be?"

She lost her smile, nodded gravely. "Yes. I could eat you up."

His grin broadened. "That doesn't sound so bad."

She put her other hand on his other shoulder, her fingers spreading out, the nails digging into his flesh. "It doesn't have to be bad. For you, especially for you, I'd want it to be sweet."

Alex started to get excited. Yet, at the same time, his dreamy dullness did not leave him. Joni's suggestive words seemed at odds with her large dark eyes, which were soft with the warm reflection from the flames. "I'm game," he said.

She nodded again. "That's how it is in the wild.

180

There is the strong and there is the game, the hunter and the hunted."

"And which am I?"

"The hunted."

Alex chuckled. "And all this time I thought I was chasing after you."

Her hands cupped the sides of his neck, squeezing into his hair. "In the beginning, I thought it could stay that way. You were different. You not only cared for me, you made me care for you. And I have never cared for anything, ever."

Alex was delighted, except that she was speaking in the past tense. "But do you still feel this way?"

Joni stopped her massage, her arms encircling his neck, her face inches away. It was then he noted the stain on her dress near her armpit. There was something about its color that he found disturbing, and he tried to pinpoint the reason.

"I feel you could've been my salvation," Joni said. "You made me feel like a girl should. I told Bala that was all I wanted. I thought he believed me. But he must have changed his mind."

"What did you and Bala do today?" Alex asked. The stain was a dirty brown, sort of crusty. He could have sworn it was a bloodstain.

"We went for a walk in the woods. Like you and I went for a walk."

"Did you go for a walk up here?" he asked, his excitement quickly turning to confusion. Joni had changed into this dress the moment she had returned to the house. This stain— Where had it come from?

"Near here."

Alex started to become aware just how firm Joni's grasp was, how strong her hands were. "Did you also go for a walk in the woods with Ray?"

"Yes," she said softly, beginning to tease her nails

lightly into the back of his neck, and not so lightly; she was actually scratching him.

"Near here?"

"Very near, Alex. I like this place. I feel at ease here."

A cold thought entered Alex's mind. It was vague, more of an unpleasant sensation than an actual idea, and yet, it seemed something he should have thought of before, something that was as obvious as hell. He began to shiver. "Joni, did you wear this dress when you went out with Ray?"

"I wore a dress. Which one doesn't matter. Alex, let me see your eyes."

He looked up, in spite of a strong desire not to; the nearness of Joni's face made it hard to think clearly. "Yes?" he mumbled.

"You're not happy."

He forced a smile. "Sure I am. It's just getting late, that's all."

She nodded. "I'm going to have to go back in a few minutes."

"Good idea," he said, shifting uncomfortably. He couldn't be sure, but it felt as though the back of his neck was bleeding. A sticky warmth was spreading around his collar. "Joni, would you stop that?"

"You're such a nice boy."

He brushed at her arms. They didn't budge an inch. "You're hurting my neck," he complained.

She leaned closer, moistening her lips as she had done on the couch just before they'd kissed. "Look at me, Alex, and it won't hurt. You'll feel like you're inside me, like you're flying."

What she said seemed almost true. He could almost forget what was going on in his body, that he even had a body, when he allowed her eyes to hold him. Almost.

God, my neck is bleeding.

Moist trails were running down his back beneath his jacket; he could feel them distinctly now, and could vividly imagine how they were staining his T-shirt, staining it the same color as the spot on Joni's white dress. The image blurred the intensity of Joni's stare, her sharp black eyes melting into a nightmare of red. "Let me go," he said.

"I can't."

"Come on, Joni, it's late."

"I want to kiss you."

"Did you feel scared when her body touched yours?"

He tried to shake free but couldn't; it was as if his neck were encircled in steel chains. His quiet anxiety instantly leapfrogged through many levels of previously unimaginable horror. Joni was stronger than he, stronger than any human being had a right to be.

"Let's kiss later," he said, shoving at her chest without effect. It was then he realized what should have been so obvious. Bala had been telling him the truth.

"Did her mouth touch yours?"

"But I need to kiss you," Joni insisted, shifting her grip from his neck to his cheeks, slowly pulling his face toward her mouth. Her lips parted slightly, and there seemed to be a dozen rows of teeth inside. Out the corner of his eyes, he could see her nails dripping bright red drops.

"No!" he shouted, searching with groping hands for anything he could use to ward her off. His fingers stumbled across a thick branch and, not realizing at first it belonged to the campfire, he whipped it up toward Joni's head. The flames had scarcely touched her hair when she let out a shout and threw him back, leaping to her feet. The base of his skull hit the ground with a force that brought stars to his eyes.

"Alex," she hissed.

He wasn't in the mood to apologize. Shaking off his dizziness, keeping a hold on his burning stick, he stood up. "What's wrong with you?" he yelled.

Joni was quick to recover from her brush with the fire. "I need you," she said, taking a step toward him.

"Why are you doing this?" he cried, taking a step backward. He would have felt better if he had the campfire between them. But it was already too late for that. She had him cut off. He could hear the river at his back. "*What* are you doing?"

"I need what that teacher spoke of, the precious ingredient. I need to get close to you."

"But you're trying to kill me!"

"Yes."

There wasn't much left of the stick he was holding. The hot end was pretty well charred; the flame flickered in his trembling grasp. He was moving away from the shelter of the cliff wall, and the wind was doing its damnest to blow the thing out. "Did you kill Ray?"

"Yes." She was closing in, her eyes as steady as the cold moonlight, the smoke from the campfire billowing around her like a witch's aura.

"Did you kill Karen?" he asked, his voice cracking.

"Yes."

"What did you do to Bala?"

"I killed him. Put down the stick, Alex."

"But then you'll kill me."

"Yes." She stopped and took a deep breath. "You should have let me kiss you. I would be done by now. I don't take long."

Ten feet beneath the heels of his shoes was Snake Tail River. There was nowhere left for him to go. "How can you be like this, Joni?" he moaned.

"By forgetting who Joni was. By letting it all come

at once, until the next time, until it comes again." She raised her right hand, her nails still dripping with the blood she had scraped from his flesh. Her eyes narrowed, and it was as though a tangible wave of insatiable hunger rolled over him. "Come to me, Alex."

A gust of wind slapped the night, and his torch died, and he was left holding ashes. Ice and ashes; it would be better than what had happened to the others. Tearing his eyes from the face he had dreamed he would always adore, he turned and jumped.

The shock of the cold was almost welcome. Her hypnotic hold on him seemed to snap. The current had him now, and though it would kill him as easily as she would have, it was not going to bleed him further.

The campfire was receding rapidly. As he resurfaced, he saw that Joni had vanished from its light. He knew his only hope was to swim to the other side, before he reached the falls. His chances were slim. He was not nearly the swimmer Bala was and the feathers lining his down jacket were already soaked, collaring him with a heavy burden. Rolling in the icy black, he fought for the zipper with freezing fingers. But when he got to it, he found the zipper jammed.

This damn jacket cost me two hundred dollars!

Submerged stones pounded his shins. Keeping his chin above the surface was consuming more of his energy than his feeble strokes. His muscles were cramping at an astonishing rate.

I can't drown. I'm supposed to be in too good shape.

He was choking on a lungful of water a minute later when he heard the scream. It seemed to emerge from every direction at once, a high, scratching screech, sharp enough to cut the bravest heart in two. He told himself that couldn't be Joni. Nothing human could make that kind of sound. Nothing living could.

But she always did sound like she had a frog in her throat.

The noise did not last, not that it mattered. He wasn't making progress. There definitely was a strong cross current preventing him from getting to the other side. And since he couldn't go back the way he had come, he was going to die. The truth of the fact rolled over him without reality. It wasn't that he couldn't picture himself dead, he just couldn't imagine Cindy at his funeral. He couldn't do that to her.

His sister was still on his mind a tumbling quarter of a mile later when he looked up and saw Joni stretching out her hand from an overhanging tree. Her eyes were on him again. There was simply no getting away from them.

"Stop, Alex," she said, and it was something of a miracle he heard her over the roar of the approaching falls. Or maybe her words were only in her mind. She was definitely inside there. He had decided with the last fiber of his being he wouldn't let her touch him again and still he accepted her offer without question, reaching out his hand to meet hers, feeling her fingers close around his with delicious warmth. He expected that she would pull him into her lap—and possibly bite his head off—but she continued to let him flail in the buffeting current.

"Alex," she said, staring down at him, her face deep with sorrow. "I really do love you."

Cindy was sitting by herself in Timber Memorial's waiting lounge when she heard the second page for her. Two hours had passed since the nurse had come to Bala's room and injected him with a solution that had sent even his extraordinary body into a deep sleep, leaving her alone with her fears. The first page had been for a call from her parents. They were still at the store, working on the inventory, her mother said. She didn't want Alex and her waiting up for them. We won't, Cindy had promised.

Alex, Alex, Alex—be on the other side of the line!

Cindy picked up the phone at the deserted nurses' station and identified herself. The hospital operator completed the connection. "Hello," Cindy said, her eyes tightly closed.

"This is Joni," the girl said without a trace of emotion.

Cindy's head dropped and she sagged against the wall. For a long moment she couldn't force a breath through her constricted throat. Joni waited patiently for her. "This is Cindy," she finally managed.

I have the rest of life to cry! But not now!

"What can I do for you, Cindy?"

She swallowed. "Is Alex there?"

"No."

"Have you seen him today?"

"Yes."

"Do you know where he is now?"

"No. Why are you at the hospital?"

Tears poured silently over her cheeks. "I'm here with Bala."

Joni considered for a moment. "Is he hurt?"

"He's slipping into a coma. He might not wake up."

"That's terrible," Joni said flatly.

Cindy hoped vultures didn't know jack about comas. "Yes, it is. But before he blacked out, I had a talk with him. We talked about some things I would like to talk with you about."

"What sort of things?"

"Shamans. Do you know much about shamans, Joni?"

Joni paused again. "When would you like to talk?"

"Tonight, in an hour. I'll meet you by the river in the park, where Bala had his accident. Is that a good spot for you?"

"Yes. Will you be alone?"

"You can bet on it."

CHAPTER
XII

CINDY WAS OUT in the parking lot when she realized she didn't have a car, neither here or at home; and the motorbike wouldn't do for what she had planned. For a moment she entertained the perverse idea of having Joni pick her up. But in the end, she went back inside the hospital and called, of all people, Jason.

"Cindy?" he said, his voice incredulous. "What do you want?"

"I want you to go to my house and pick up Wolf, Sybil, a pair of binoculars, and that rifle we took up to the waterfall. You know where we keep the key. Wolf and Sybil are in the house. The gun and binoculars are in the garage. Also, get me a box of shells. You'll find them in one of the workbench drawers."

"You've got to be kidding."

"I want you to bring the pets and the stuff to Memorial. I'm here now. Oh, and I'm going to have to borrow your car. Bring the Camaro."

"Cindy, have you flipped? You're trying to put me in jail. Why should I help you?"

"If you help me now, maybe you won't go to jail. Understand?"

He sounded doubtful, but interested. "What are you up to?"

"None of your business. But if you're not here in less than half an hour, my offer expires."

Jason could be reasonable when it suited him. After repeating her shopping list back to her, he hung up with a promise to be there in twenty minutes. Cindy waited on the front steps of the hospital and watched the full moon rise higher and higher in the sky. The power of Joni's eyes were on her mind. Perhaps she should have told Jason to fetch her sunglasses. It was too late now.

Jason was true to his word. She waved for him to keep the engine running when he pulled into the emergency unloading zone not long aferward. Wolf barked hello out the backseat window as she jogged down the steps to the red Camaro. She didn't give Jason a chance to ask questions. She didn't even offer to give him a ride home. Handing him the keys to the cycle, she scooted him out of the front seat and slid behind the wheel, making a quick check to see that he had brought everything. Sybil was sitting quietly in her cage in the passenger seat, her sightless eyes watching her.

"Joni," the bird said.

"Don't you know it," Cindy swore, hitting the accelerator without saying good-bye to her old boyfriend.

She had a fairly good idea of where Joni must have thrown Bala over the cliff. He had spoken of Lot H, and of the path they had taken that cut directly through the woods to the river. That was rough terrain down there in the gorge, beneath the falls.

I should've told her two hours. I should've been early.

It was on the ride up to the park that the fear began to hit her. Her plan could be nothing but an elaborate suicide, made in haste before she'd really thought about what it was she was doing. Although she already missed Alex terribly, she didn't want to die. The steering wheel began to slip under her sweaty fingers, and she gripped it all the harder to keep her hands from shaking. All of a sudden she realized just how fragile a thing it was to be alive, to have your lungs breathing air, your heart pumping blood. If Joni was as strong as Bala said, she would only have to get a hand on her, a finger even, and Cindy Jones would be history. Bala was part Bairavee and the witch had swatted him as if he were a fly.

"Her head had also suffered from what appeared to be an extremely powerful blow—the top of her skull was cracked in several places."

A quarter of a mile down the mountain from Lot H, Cindy parked. With the giant moon and the howling wind, the silver trees jostling with each other in wild rhythms, the forest appeared possessed with an alien presence. Taking a string Alex always kept handy on the floor of the bird cage, she tied one end to Sybil's right leg, fastening the other end around a gold necklace Alex had given her for her birthday. Wolf watched the whole operation with the utmost curiosity.

"I'm going to be counting on you tonight, boy," she said, finishing with the bird and petting the dog on the head. It took her only a minute to load the rifle.

She was late but she took the hike up the road slowly, hugging the trees, staying in the shadows. Wolf's company was reassuring, and she kept a tight hold on his leash while the yellow parrot rode serenely on her right shoulder. Yet she was having trouble breathing, and she couldn't stop glancing above her, at the sky; she kept expecting a huge vulture to swoop down upon her.

Alex's car was sitting in the middle of the parking lot. Cindy considered leaving her cover to peek through the windows. What stopped her, more than the fear Joni would spot her, was the possibility she might find Alex's body inside.

My beautiful brother.

She didn't take the path Bala had described, but rather, continued to climb higher, until she came to a second path that she knew also led to the river. She wanted to come upon Joni unaware.

The waterfall was above and off to her right as she crept cautiously forward, and the rocky vale resounded with the noise of its white water. The path she was on was seldom traveled. Branches scratched at her arms and legs, and also at the barrel of her rifle, which she held low in front, her finger on the trigger. Bala hadn't commented on Joni's hearing and Cindy prayed it wasn't as extraordinary as her grip. The dried branches felt like so many claws trying to get under her skin.

"It looked as though her head had been grabbed by the ears and squashed together."

Whatever happened, she didn't want that damn reporter trying to describe what was left of her body.

A few minutes later she reached the end of the trees and was granted a wide view of the gorge. Crouching down behind a boulder, Wolf breathing on the side of her face, she spanned the area of the supposed meeting spot with her binoculars. It was only after a close search that she saw Joni. The girl was sitting approximately half a mile away, two hundred feet below, in the shadow of a sheer overhanging ledge, on a smooth stone a few feet from the water. If not for Joni's white dress, Cindy probably would have missed her.

"Bitch," she whispered.

Having Joni in view allowed her to relax somewhat. Joni's decision to wait away from the trees appeared to be a serious tactical mistake. Even in the shadow, she made a respectable target. Carefully, Cindy began to work her way closer, weaving around the jagged rocks and dry shrubs, watching where she placed her feet. The whole time Joni sat as still as a statue.

When she was perhaps two football fields away, Cindy again went down on her knees behind a boulder. Her father kept the scope on the rifle well adjusted, and as she centered Joni's chest between the crosshairs, the barrel propped steadily across the stone, she knew all she had to do was pull the trigger and all the sheaths and all their owners in Timber would be safe. But she hesitated, and suddenly there were so many reasons why she should. It made no difference that the reasons contradicted each other.

First, she wanted to personally confront Joni. The girl had killed her brother, and she wanted her to know, wanted her to *see* what was coming before the bullet cut her down. The reason was savage and illogical and that made it all the stronger.

Second, she was worried about the police. Bala had commented about going to jail, and when you got right down to it, she probably would be tried for murder if she pulled the trigger. Nowadays, a slug could be traced back to practically any gun. Plus good old reliable Jason could always reverse the tables and act as a witness against her.

Third, her disgust at Bala's inability to deal with Joni had been unfair. It *was* next to impossible to believe the gorgeous creature resting on the boulder was evil. Joni even looked sad. Cindy took her eye off the scope. Her father's deep repugnance at the killing of any living creature was with her, and couldn't be ignored.

And finally, there was her brilliant plan that could

satisfy all these objections to wasting Joni, and still get rid of the menace. Shouldering the rifle, she decided she would have to try it.

Her brilliant plan had one major flaw. It would probably get her killed.

Cindy stood, stepping gingerly toward the base of the cliff where Joni waited. Halfway there, she stopped and undid Wolf's leash, whispering in the dog's ear.

"You're to stay, Wolf. Stay."

The dog did as told. But if all went as planned, he would disobey her command within minutes.

Grandfather Bairavee, if you can be more than one place at the same time, please be here with me now. Please help me.

Petting the dog one last time, she started down.

Joni glanced up as Cindy waded through the shallow pool that was the final barrier between them, the icy water pouring over Cindy's high-top sneakers. Since Joni was still cloaked by the shadow, Cindy felt it should be safe to look directly at her. She could barely even see Joni's eyes, never mind be swept away by them. So she thought.

But before she could confront Joni, something off to her left caught her attention. Stuck in the water between a stick and a stone was Alex's jacket. The back had been torn to shreds.

No, no, no, no . . .

The will to live went out of her then, but not the fear of death. Her entire body began to shiver worse than when Bala had fished her from the cold river that now flowed at her back. Sybil stirred restlessly beside her head. Cindy tried to raise her rifle, tried to look at Joni and not see her. "Where's Alex?" she whispered.

Joni sighed, stretching her legs over the rock. "You know where he is."

"Did you kill him?"

"Yes."

A single powerful tremor went through her. "Why did you kill him?"

Joni slid effortlessly off the boulder, standing upright, glanced briefly in the direction Cindy had come from. "Didn't Bala tell you why?"

"He told me you're a vulture."

Joni took a casual step forward, the hair around her head a part of the inky black from which she was emerging. "I'm more than that, Cindy. I'm much more than that."

Cindy blinked several times. There was something obstructing her vision, as if a smoky haze were arising from the ground between them. Her breathing difficulty returned, and she began to pant rapidly. The air was full of strange odors, of things rotting. "You're nothing, Joni. You're dead meat."

"I saw you up there a few minutes ago, Cindy," she said, her approach steady but unhurried. "I think you could have shot me then. But I think you were afraid to. I could sense your fear."

"I'm not afraid," Cindy whispered, lying. This *thing* had killed God knew how many people, torn them to pieces so that their own families couldn't recognize them. Suddenly she realized the fool she had been to challenge Joni in this lonely spot. Suddenly she had no idea what she was supposed to do next.

This is a spell!

Hadn't Bala also been caught in an instant?

"But you are, you're scared you're going to die. And you are going to die. Or I am. We both can't live. You see, I'm scared, too. Bala probably didn't tell you that. I'm only trying to survive." She stepped out of the shadow, her white face appearing as lifeless as polished marble. "Look at me, Cindy."

Cindy looked; it was impossible not to. Not even the knowledge that it was her death to do so could make her stop. An invisible claw seemed to stretch out from Joni, enfolding Cindy from head to toe. Then the spell took a twist, coming at her from the inside rather than the outside. Cindy could no longer see Joni's eyes. But she could see *through* them. A swollen orange moon filled her universe, a moon from long ago, glimpsed from inside another body, a full moon hanging in a desert sky above a parched land too dry for even a vulture's empty thoughts.

Cindy's consciousness fragmented. There were three of her, and one of them was not human. Images of her life in the Wyoming Rockies, of a young girl's days in the English countryside, and of a beastly existence on the hungry plains of Africa bombarded her like a swirling kaleidoscope, the latter's memories convulsing her stomach in nausea. *She* remembered chewing on bloody fly-soaked carcasses!

I'm not dying. I'm being possessed.

But through all these memories was the moon, seen from different perspectives, but nevertheless remaining the same. Tilting her head back, she could see it still, and it seemed her only thread to reality. Different moments in time and space converged. As a vulture she had acute eyesight. She could see the craters of the moon without aid. And even though as a young girl she'd used binoculars, she'd thought the same as the vulture, *that it was full of holes*. And this single point in common created a single hole in the trance, a place where she could stand and not be bewitched.

Shoot the moon, Cindy. It's your only safe target.

Safe for all of them.

Cindy raised the rifle and shot the moon.

The roar of the gun came to her from far off.

Cindy came back to her body exactly where she had left it. Only now Joni was no longer fifteen feet away, but standing inches from her face, her black eyes twin silver mirrors of the moon above, her breath as cold as frost.

"Yes, I've always watched the sky," Joni said softly. "I watched it believing it was home, that I would one day return there." She raised her right hand, caught a lock of Cindy's hair, and slowly began to curl it around her finger. "Time for you to go home."

Cindy tasted blood in her mouth. She had bit her lip. "No," she pleaded.

"Don't resist me."

"Please."

"It hurts much more that way." Joni snapped her hand away, ripping the lock of hair from Cindy's scalp, sending a shearing pain slicing through her head, warm blood dripping round her ear. Sybil sat silent, unmoving. "It's like getting eaten alive."

"Don't, please." Cindy wept.

Joni smiled, cupping Cindy's chin in her hand. "You loved your brother, but you don't love me. I can't take you for my own. Don't cry, Cindy. It will be all right." Joni's fingers tightened, her nails pressing into Cindy's bones. "I will simply kill you."

Cindy squeezed her eyes shut, as Joni raised the other hand, placing it on the back of Cindy's skull, and began to squeeze the life out of her body.

Then there was a second roar in the night, unlike the sound of the rifle, but every bit as deadly. It had been part of Cindy's plan that the gunshot would have called him, and perhaps it had and he'd had difficulty navigating the steep rocky yards that separated them. Or maybe he had only thought to strike when he had seen Joni take hold of her. Whatever the case, Wolf was now attacking.

The bone-crushing pressure ceased. Cindy opened her eyes. Joni had leapt a dozen feet away, her soul-sucking eyes darting from her to the dog, back and forth. Wolf was less than fifty feet up the hill and closing fast. And as though their minds were still fused, Cindy could understand Joni's thoughts. She could take a few seconds to kill the dog, and leave Cindy free to put a bullet in her chest, or she could try to kill Cindy quickly, and leave the dog free to rip her throat out.

Joni had seen Wolf attack Jason when he had fired the gun, but Joni knew Wolf was never going to attack his master.

There's a way out, Joni. Take it! Take it!

Planting her right knee and using it to support the rifle, Cindy aimed directly at Joni's heart. Joni's attention continued to flash back and forth between her and the dog. A decision was going to have to be made fast. With all the noise and excitement, Sybil began to rock nervously. Joni appeared to become aware of the bird for the first time.

"Joni," Cindy said.

"Joni Jones," the bird chirped.

Joni's eyes suddenly settled in their direction. She nodded slightly, going very still.

Cindy quickly shut her eyes.

Sybil stopped her rocking.

Something brushed past Cindy's head, a cool mist that could be felt but never seen; the stuff of ghosts and spirits.

Sybil began to flap violently, trying to fly away, not succeeding. Cindy opened her eyes. "Heel, Wolf!" she shouted. "Heel!"

Her dog, making ready to leap, stalled in midstride. The command had hit home. Or maybe he'd halted because his prey had suddenly given up. Joni lay collapsed on the ground.

"Stay, stay," Cindy told Wolf, climbing to her feet, approaching Joni cautiously, keeping her finger on the rifle trigger, Sybil continuing to struggle for freedom on her shoulder. Wolf leaned over and licked Joni's peaceful face, half-hidden beneath her beautiful black hair. The girl was not breathing. Cindy knelt and felt at her neck for a pulse.

"My grandfather said Joni was dead."

The question was settled now. There was no pulse.

Cindy pulled her necklace over her head, worried that Sybil would scratch her face, and pinned the parrot to the ground with the help of a heavy rock set across the string attached to the bird's ankle. Then she looked around for something to do and realized there was nothing she could do. All the monsters had been slain. The genie was back in her bottle.

And my brother is gone.

Cindy rested her face on Joni's side and began to cry softly, not just for Alex, but for the others as well, including Joni Harper.

Time went by—ten minutes, perhaps an hour. Cindy finally stirred, as though awakening from a dream, and sat up, Wolf nudging her cheek with his wet nose. Wrapping her arm around the dog, she wondered if she had the strength left to walk to the car, if she should even bother.

A sound at her back made her whirl.

A panting young man limped around the bend, coming toward her, a huge stick in his hand. Cindy reached for her rifle. "What do you want?" she called.

"I'd like a ride home, if you've got one."

"Alex? Alex!"

"It's me."

Joni got me after all. I've died and gone over to the other side.

Cindy didn't care if that turned out to be the truth. In her excitement, she tried to jump up without realizing her soggy feet had gone to sleep while she had lain against Joni. She ended up flat on her face, laughing hysterically. "Alex, you're not dead!"

"I never said I was," he said, dragging through the puddle of water, using his stick as a cane. He stopped above her, dripping wet. "I'd offer you my hand but I think my leg's broken."

"What's a little broken leg?" she asked, making no sense and not caring. How was she ever going to thank God for this one? She would probably have to become a nun or something. "Sit down and tell me what happened!"

He accepted her invitation, except he sat next to Joni instead of herself, touching the fallen girl's hair. "Somehow, this doesn't surprise me," he said sadly.

Cindy stopped smiling. "I'm sorry, Alex."

He was silent for a moment. A single tear ran over his cheek. "Yeah."

Cindy put her hand on his back. "Who would have thought it would end this way."

Alex looked at her. "When did you find out about her—her—?" He didn't know what to say.

"Bala told me this evening."

Alex was surprised. "Then he's all right?"

"He's in the hospital, but he'll heal."

"Good." Alex turned back to Joni. "What did he tell you?"

Cindy hesitated. The whole truth might not be the best thing for him right now, if ever. "About a year ago, Bala's grandfather performed a shamic experiment using Joni. It sort of ended badly." She paused. "Was she rough on you?"

Alex glanced up at the moon, then at his torn jacket stuck in the water, shaking his head. "Not as rough as the waterfall was."

"You went over the *falls*? That's impossible."

"I should have died," Alex agreed, touching Joni's head again. "I should have died twice. I was in the river, and she was hanging on to me from that log Jason used when trying to rescue you. I knew if she pulled me out of the river, she would kill me. It was like she wouldn't be able to help herself. And she knew it, too, and didn't want to do it."

"What happened?"

Alex smiled for a moment, then lowered his head. "She told me she loved me. And she held my eyes, and it was like she gave me a part of herself. I'm not sure if she actually said these words, but I remember them. 'Fly, Alex, you can fly.'" He took his hand away from Joni. "When I went over the waterfall, I seemed to fall forever. And when I hit, it didn't feel that hard." He shrugged. "But I still broke my leg. I guess now I've got a good excuse for not winning the next race."

Cindy hugged him. "Maybe you did fly."

And maybe she did love you. Maybe not all of Joni was taken that terrible day.

Alex noticed for the first time that Joni had not bled. "I heard a shot," he said, frowning. "I thought—how did you stop her?"

Cindy stood and carefully removed the rock that kept her brother's parrot from flying away, replacing the necklace and the attached string around her neck. Settling on her shoulder, Sybil stopped fussing. "Tell the police you fell off this ledge and broke your leg," she said. "And when Joni ran down here and saw you lying on the rocks, she must have thought you were dead. Tell them she just keeled over. There isn't a mark on her body. I can corroborate your story. They'll believe us."

"But what really happened?"

Neither Alex or herself could carry the body back; they would have to send the police for it. Ignoring the cold, Cindy removed her coat and gently covered Joni, thinking of the strong-willed girl Bala had described, who wanted to see some magic, and who saw more than she had bargained for. "That *is* what happened, Alex. She got scared. And it killed her."

EPILOGUE

*I*T WAS A DAY for funerals, and it seemed all wrong she was having to worry about what she was going to wear. But the reality of the situation was that she simply didn't have the clothes for it; most of her things were bright colors. Flipping through her wardrobe for the third time, she decided her gray pants suit was her best bet, even though it needed pressing. Once, Ray had told her she looked like a *real woman* in the outfit.

There was a knock at her bedroom door. "Are you decent?" Alex called.

"I'm stark naked, just a sec," she called back, reaching for her yellow robe. Her hair was still wet from her shower. "Come in."

Alex had a midthigh-high cast on his left leg that he wasn't letting *anybody* sign. Their mother had had to split his dress pants to get him inside them. He lumbered into the room and plopped down on her bed. "You look clean," he said, meaning she had used up all the hot water and that their mother was complaining.

"I not only look it, I smell it. How much time have we got?"

"Ten minutes, at the most. Don't bother with makeup."

Cindy picked up her lipstick, facing the mirror above her chest-of-drawers. "Ray always liked a woman who knew how to fix herself up." She noted Alex was carrying the morning paper. "Does Mr. Cooke have another *mystery* article for us?"

"How did you know?"

"Let's just say I didn't have to use my psychic abilities to figure it out."

Alex opened the paper on his lap. "You might want to read it. Our names are mentoned twice on the front page."

Cindy took the paper and glanced at the article.

HOW DID JONI HARPER DIE?

She tossed the paper in the waste basket by her desk, muttering, "I could've sworn he used the same title a couple of weeks ago."

"You're not going to read it?"

"Nope."

"Why not?"

"Why should I?"

Alex nodded, looked uncomfortable. "I need your advice."

"Take the money."

Now he was puzzled. "How did you know Ray willed me money?"

She messed up her lipstick. "I didn't, I was just being silly. What was Ray doing with a will?"

"His mom said he made it up as a practical joke. But now the thing is supposed to be legally binding."

"How much did he leave you?"

"His mother wasn't sure. It's a five-gallon water bottle stuffed with change. He'd been collecting it since he was a kid."

"Is it mostly quarters?"

"Cindy!"

"Just wondering. So what's your problem? Do you need help putting it in paper rolls so the bank will take it?"

Alex shook his head impatiently. "Mrs. Bower just called and said Ray had requested that I, Alex Jones, take care of the disposal of his remains."

"What? Didn't his mother have him cremated?" She knew Mrs. Lee had had Joni's body cremated. Having lived with the strange girl for a couple of months, the poor woman had probably been having nightmares of vampires. Cindy wouldn't have been surprised.

The funerals were actually simple memorial services, and no one would be going out to the cemetery. Cindy thought it was a nice touch that they were being held together.

"Yes, he was cremated. That's the problem. Ray wanted me to get rid of his ashes."

"What did he want you to do with them?"

Alex sighed. "He wanted me to mix them in with the chalk we use to mark off the cross-country course. He said in the will he liked the idea of all us guys on the team stomping on him all year."

Cindy smiled. "That's classic. Are you going to do it?"

"I'll get the chalk all dirty!"

"Nah. The stuff's bright gold, right? I bet you'll hardly be able to tell the difference."

Alex was unconvinced. "This whole idea is gross. I couldn't ever tell anybody."

"Well, you're good at keeping secrets."

He changed the subject. "While you were in the shower, Jason called."

Cindy hunted around for her blow dryer. "I hope you told him if he calls again I'll invent another nasty rumor to attach to his dirty name."

"You're not going to call him back?"

"Nope."

"He said he wanted to apologize."

"That guy's going to be apologizing for the rest of his screwy life."

Alex shrugged, standing. "Have it your way. Oh, Bala's downstairs."

"You kidding? Why didn't you tell me?"

"He just got here."

"Send him up."

"Don't you want to get dressed first?"

"He's still got his cast, too, doesn't he?"

"Yeah."

"Then what are you worried about? I should be safe. Send him up. And quit looking at me like that."

Alex gestured to the bird cage beside her bed. "Why are you keeping Sybil up here?"

Cindy stopped. "Do you mind? Lately, I've just felt like having her around, you know?"

Alex didn't understand, and didn't know it, and she wasn't going to explain herself. "Has she learned to say your name yet?" he asked.

"Not yet."

"As long as you feed her, it's fine with me." He moved for the door.

"Alex? How long do parrots live?"

He paused. "Some stay around over a hundred years."

"But Sybil was old when you got her, right?"

"Yeah. Why?"

"I was just wondering." She studied his face, concerned. He hadn't spoken much since that night. "Are you going to be all right today?"

"I don't mind remembering her," he said quietly. "There's very little that I need to forget."

She nodded. "We'll sit together."

Before Bala arrived, she quickly slipped on underwear beneath her robe. This would be, after all, the first time he had been in her room.

And the last time?

Like Alex, he knocked before entering. He had to lower his head to get through the door. His left arm was in a cast and sling and he appeared to have the ribs beneath his navy blue sweatshirt taped; there was a general stiffness in the way he moved—quite a change for him.

"I did not know you were dressing," he said shyly, averting his eyes. She laughed.

"Hey, you can look at me. I'm not naked."

He did so reluctantly, blushing. "I could wait downstairs."

"No, you have to stay. Sit on my bed. I'm glad you're here. I'm surprised that doctor let you out this soon. What's it been, three days?"

Bala sat, his legs reaching from the end of the bed to the wall. "Four, if you count Monday."

"That's right, today's Friday," she muttered. It went without saying that almost the whole week had gone by and she hadn't visited him. Sure, she'd called, but she knew he'd wait to see her before asking certain questions, ones she didn't want to answer. "How's your arm?"

"I am healing swiftly."

"I bet you are," she said thoughtfully.

Bala searched her face. "I did not think I would see you again when I awoke and learned from Mrs. Lee that you had gone to meet with Joni."

Cindy forced a laugh. "I'm a hard person to get rid of." Then she caught herself, softening her tone. "I suppose that isn't very funny. I had the same thought myself." She leaned against her desk, smoothed her hands over her legs. "But we're both here now and I suppose that's all that matters."

He nodded, spoke with feeling. "You look good, Cindy."

It was her turn to blush. "Alex just told me I looked clean."

"What I meant—"

"I know what you meant," she interrupted, looking him straight in the eye. "Thank you. I don't know if you have any idea how long I've been wondering if you thought I was attractive. I think you look good, too. Great, in fact." Then the question just burst out. "Are you leaving to go back home?"

"Yes."

She chewed on her lip. This pain in the heart didn't get any easier the more you experienced it. The pain just got worse. "Do you have to?" she asked, her voice quivering.

"I must tell my grandfather about Joni."

"Couldn't you write him?"

Bala glanced around the room. "I was wrong about him, about what he knows. It is all real. And he is getting old, and if he is going to teach me what I need to know, then it should not be delayed."

"You're going to become a shaman?"

He smiled faintly at the note of approval in her tone. "I would let you call me a magician."

To her immense embarrassment, she began to cry. The tears had a mind of their own and wouldn't stop, even when she held her arm across her eyes. Bala stood and tentatively reached out to touch her. She responded by burying her face in his chest, hugging him gently with both her arms. "Will I see you again?" she asked.

He ran the finger of his right hand through her wet hair. "On my eighth birthday I asked my grandfather how big the world was. When you are small, he said, it is huge. But when you are a master of nature, it is like a ball you can hold in your hand." He pressed his hand to the side of her head. "We will see each other again, Cindy, even if we have to meet in a dream."

She leaned back, looking up, still holding on to him. "I guess now I'll have something to look forward to when I go to sleep at night."

"I hope you recognize me in my true colors. I may not be the great warrior you once thought I was."

She hugged him again. "Don't say that. I didn't know what I was talking about in the hospital. You did what you could. You faced her alone. You're the bravest person I've ever met."

"Next to you." Then he asked *the* question. "How did you do it, Cindy?"

She closed her eyes. "I can't tell you."

"You do not know?"

She let go of him, wiped at her cheeks, and stepped to the window from where she could see the distant waterfall. "I gave her a choice. That's all I can say, Bala. Please don't ask me why."

He accepted that. "I will not be going to the service. I am afraid too many people associate me with the deaths. I never did give the police a clear account of what happened to me. I thought it would be best to just take a bus to the airport. There is a flight that leaves this afternoon. I have my things and I have already said good-bye to Pam and Mrs. Alta."

A faint rainbow had formed across the face of the waterfall, as sometimes happened when the light was right, and yet, it did not look beautiful to her. It just looked cold. "I'm glad I got a chance to say good-bye," she said softly, feeling sorry for herself.

Hey, if I don't tell him now, he'll never know.

Cindy suddenly turned and, inching up on her toes, kissed him warmly, catching him by surprise. "I'm counting on more than just a dream, Bala," she told him. "You're going to have to do better than that."

When he was gone, and she was finished getting dressed, she realized she hadn't given Sybil her breakfast. Picking up the feed jar, she leaned over the cage and stared at the bird.

She could have sworn it stared back.

"How long do parrots live?"

It was true she'd given Joni a choice, but it had been Bala who'd given her the choices, though he might not realize that until he was back with his grandfather. While lying in the hospital bed, he had told her he was certain the creature in Joni's body couldn't be a bird anymore. Then he had indirectly contradicted himself a few minutes later when explaining how she had immobilized him.

"She turned and stared at me. Her large black eyes seemed to fill the world. Having been shown the way to leave her body once, she apparently had not forgotten how to leave it again. This must be how she gets a grip on an individual's sheath; she lets a portion of herself wrap around the person."

Obviously, the spirit in Joni knew how to get around. The key, Cindy had realized, was to put her in a situation where she would *decide* to go into another body. And that was what Cindy had done, forcing the vulture to opt for a new landlord by placing her between a wild dog and a loaded gun.

Alex had told her the afternoon after his big date that he hadn't explained Sybil's blindness to Joni. He'd been afraid Joni would feel sorry for the bird.

Sightless eyes. You could go in, if you knew how,

but you could never get out. No matter how long you lived.

And what happened to you, Sybil? Were you just shoved aside, out into the cold?

"Joni," the bird said.

"I know," Cindy whispered. Had Alex not convinced her Joni really had loved him, that there really had been a portion of the original soul behind those beautiful eyes, she would've drowned the parrot. Certainly, if Bala had been told the truth, he would have insisted the bird be destroyed.

And now she was afraid to let the thing out of her sight. It was like the bird had cast a spell on her.

Sometimes she wondered if she wasn't taking a chance.

"Cindy," the bird said.

Sometimes she wondered if the bird was completely blind.

ABOUT THE AUTHOR

CHRISTOPHER PIKE was born in Brooklyn, New York, but grew up in Los Angeles, where he lives to this day. Prior to becoming a writer, he worked in a factory, painted houses, and programmed computers. His hobbies include astronomy, meditating, running, playing with his nieces and nephews, and making sure his books are prominently displayed in local bookstores. He is the author of *Last Act, Spellbound, Gimme a Kiss, Final Friends I, II,* and *III* (all available from Archway Paperbacks). He has also writen *Slumber Party, Weekend, Chain Letter, The Tachyon Web,* and *Sati,* an adult novel about a very unusual young lady.

FROM THE BESTSELLING AUTHOR OF
SLUMBER PARTY AND *CHAIN LETTER*

Christopher Pike

No one does it better than Christopher Pike. His mystery and suspense novels are so fast-paced and gripping that they're guaranteed to keep you on the edge of your seat, guessing whodunit...

Join Christopher Pike as he opens up a whole new world of mystery and excitement for you.

LAST ACT

A group of seniors at Care High are putting on a play about a murder. On opening night one of the leading actresses is shot. Melanie—another actress—must smoke out the real killer, before he or she kills again!

SPELLBOUND

Cindy Jones, a senior at Timber High, has the perfect life. Only one thing clouds her sunny horizon—the mysterious murder of her boyfriend's old girlfriend. Cindy has to unravel this terrifying mystery or no teenager will be safe!

COMING IN JULY—*GIMME A KISS*

___ **LAST ACT**	64980/$2.75	
___ **SPELLBOUND**	64979/$2.75	

**Simon & Schuster Mail Order Dept. CPS
200 Old Tappan Rd., Old Tappan, N.J. 07675**

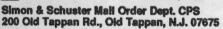